A Rogue to Forget

Rogues of the Lowlands
Book Two

By
Hildie McQueen

Text by Hildie McQueen
Cover by Dar Albert

Dragonblade Publishing, Inc. is an imprint of Kathryn Le Veque Novels, Inc.
P.O. Box 23
Moreno Valley, CA 92556
ceo@dragonbladepublishing.com

Produced in the United States of America

First Edition September 2023
Trade Paperback Edition

ARE YOU SIGNED UP FOR DRAGONBLADE'S BLOG?

You'll get the latest news and information on exclusive giveaways, exclusive excerpts, coming releases, sales, free books, cover reveals and more.

Check out our complete list of authors, too!

No spam, no junk. That's a promise!

Sign Up Here

www.dragonbladepublishing.com

Dearest Reader;

Thank you for your support of a small press. At Dragonblade Publishing, we strive to bring you the highest quality Historical Romance from some of the best authors in the business. Without your support, there is no 'us', so we sincerely hope you adore these stories and find some new favorite authors along the way.

Happy Reading!

CEO, Dragonblade Publishing

Additional Dragonblade Books by Author Hildie McQueen

Rogues of the Lowlands Series

A Rogue to Reform (Book 1)

A Rogue to Forget (Book 2)

Clan Ross Series

A Heartless Laird

A Hardened Warrior

A Hellish Highlander

A Flawed Scotsman

A Fearless Rebel

A Fierce Archer

A Haunted Scot (Novella)

Highland Knight (Novella)

Stones of Ard Cairn (Novella)

The Lyon's Den Series

The Lyon's Laird

Pirates of Britannia Series

The Sea Lord

The Sea Lyon

De Wolfe Pack: The Series

The Duke's Fiery Bride

CHAPTER ONE

Glasgow, Scotland
April, 1823

THE SOUNDS OF the night were interesting, Henry Campbell pondered as he headed home. His horse nickered, probably complaining at being out at such late an hour. As he went past the now closed Kerr Tea Shop, he could not help but recall the last time he'd entered the front doors.

It was a gathering place for those out and about who required refreshment and perhaps a pastry. There always seemed to be a table open amidst the busy place and a warm and friendly smile from whomever came to serve.

At this late hour, the shop would have been closed; however, it was obvious it was abandoned now.

Devoid of light.

Devoid of life.

Two weeks earlier

THE TRYST HAD been enjoyable enough that Henry reluctantly left the woman's bed. It was a hard rule that he never spent the night. Lingering after what was a casual assignation could bring about expectations. No matter what, he preferred never to hurt a woman who willingly shared her body with him.

As he rode up to Kerr Tea Shop, he noted that, although it was much too late now for the business to be open, the front door was thrown open and a dim light flickered inside. Something felt wrong.

Riding past, Henry tried to look inside; the only thing he could see were the outlines of the chairs and tables. If someone was inside working late, they should not have left the door open. Finally, he pulled the horse to a stop, all the while convincing himself there was absolutely nothing wrong.

After tethering the horse, he stood outside and looked around the deserted street. There was no harm in ensuring nothing was amiss. Once he did that, he'd close the door and inform the owner the next day of the mishap.

His footsteps echoed and the wind blew, tickling the back of his neck, seeming to send a warning of danger. Not one to ignore a premonition, Henry bent and pulled a dagger from his boot. Considering that the owner, John Kerr, would be there working late and he didn't wish to scare him, Henry kept the dagger hidden in his cuff.

The blade would be accessible in case the shop was being vandalized and robbed and the intruder remained. Given the silence, he doubted it, but it never hurt to be prepared.

When Henry entered cautiously through the open door, the front area looked to be unperturbed. Without the clatter of dishes and din of conversation, it felt like a different place. Still, the pleasant aroma of coffee and baked goods hung in the air.

"Anyone here?" Henry called out. There was silence.

Lifting the glass of a lantern on a back table, he lit the wick and instantly the dimness was lessened. He scanned the room, ensuring to keep his back to the door, and found everything in its place. Nothing had been broken. It was eerily silent.

"Is someone here?" Henry called out again, and continued to the back where the only light in the entire place had emanated from.

His footsteps seemed to echo with each step as he made his way back, expecting someone to appear at any moment.

Preferring to be prepared, he'd pulled the dagger from his cuff, holding it out, and continued ever-so-slowly through the second doorway.

Slumped over in a chair was a man he recognized as Mister Kerr, the owner of the tea shop.

"Mister Kerr?" Henry approached the slumbering man. "Mister Kerr." He jostled the man to wake him. "Are you unwell?"

It was then the metallic smell emanated and Henry saw the dark puddle of blood under the man's head and neck.

The man's throat had been sliced open.

Immediately, Henry had stuck his dagger back into his boot. The last thing he needed was to be blamed for killing a man he'd only met once or twice and, as far as he could recall, never held a conversation with.

Despite not knowing the man, sadness at what occurred enveloped him as he rushed back outside, mounting his horse, and went in search of someone to help. Luckily, two constables stood two streets over and had hurried to the scene.

After alerting the authorities, he'd been the one to give both the mother and daughter the bad news. It had been a horrible evening, the memories of their heartbreak strong in his mind.

It had been especially painful to break the news to Hannah Kerr, the man's daughter, who he'd made friends with.

A rider approached and shook Henry out of his musings. It didn't do to be distracted when riding through the city at such a late hour. It left one open to be robbed or attacked.

The two passed each other without a word or acknowledgement.

Henry recognized the man who was married and father to two daughters who'd recently been introduced into society. The man obviously did not wish to be seen riding in the vicinity of a well-known house of ill repute, so he pulled his hat down and averted his face as he rode past.

It mattered not to Henry what the man did; he did not particularly care for him, as the man was ruthless. A banker, who took little pity when ruining someone's life by withdrawing support or calling loans. What did bother Henry was the fact that the man would go home and lay next to his wife.

He never understood how married men could do such a thing.

Finally, his family estate came into view. His family home was grand by society standards; his father had not only inherited a huge family fortune but had amassed additional wealth by investing and sponsoring businesses. And although not titled, they were held in high esteem by members of high society. Something Henry did not give a fig about.

"Ah, there you see, we are almost home," he said to the horse, which quickened its pace. Henry chuckled. "I apologize for the late hour."

Upon arriving at the mansion that was his home, Henry rode to the stables and went about unsaddling his horse and preparing the animal for the evening. He filled the oat bucket and ensured there was fresh water for his steed before he was finally able to head to bed.

Entering through the kitchen entrance, he hesitated for a moment, considering if he should grab something to eat. There was a loaf of bread on the table that was covered with a clean cloth. No doubt it was to be used for breakfast. He sliced a piece of bread, retrieved a glass of milk, and quickly devoured the simple meal.

The darkness of his bedchamber was doused when he lit a lamp and went about undressing in preparation for bed.

There was much to do the next day. For one, he would meet with his father and ask for a larger monthly stipend.

Secondly, Henry had to formulate a plan to come up with the funding for his portion of an investment he'd agreed to be part of.

He'd left his wayward ways in the past and began working with his father doing what he could to rebuild the trust that had been lost after he'd squandered a small fortune in the gambling dens of Glasgow.

No longer the reckless gambler who'd relied on his father to cover his gaming debts, Henry carried the burden of guilt and promised himself that when his investment paid off, the first thing he would do would be to repay his father every single cent.

The investment amount he required was large, a sum he did not currently have. Somehow, in the next few weeks, he had to come up with the money.

He and three friends had discussed and wagered that the quickest way was to seduce a wealthy woman and convince her to give them the needed capital.

Laying on the bed, hands behind his head, Henry considered that most of the women he knew were quite astute. As much fun as it was to consider convincing someone to hand over such a great sum, it would be no easy task.

With his family connections, he could easily marry a young lass whose dowry would undoubtedly cover the sum he needed. However, it was a huge step to take for capital.

The ship would be sailing in a few weeks, and he had to figure out what to do. He would not be the one to let his friends down. The investment would return tenfold to those who funded the vessel, and he would do anything to be a sponsor.

It was the only way to repay his debts to his father and become self-reliant.

"I DID NOT expect to see you up so early." His father's greeting had a note of annoyance. "You were not at the evening meal, and I suspect you arrived home quite late…again."

Henry lifted the cup of tea to his lips and met his father's gaze. "Indeed I did. But I am here prepared to work. As I've told you, Father, I wish to learn as much as I can from working alongside you. I have a sponsorship pending and another business venture I am considering. I do not wish to make any mistakes."

At his statement, his father's brows rose in surprise. "I would like to hear more about these businesses you plan to be part of."

"It is so good to hear you two discussing your day. It is the way it should be," his mother said with a curious expression. "I for one am more interested in ensuring you give me a list of whom you'd like to invite to the gathering next week." Her gaze pinned first her husband and then Henry. "You have both agreed it is a grand idea to host an event here."

"Mother I only have three good friends and you know who they are. I cannot think of anyone else to add to my list." Henry began eating, sure his mother would insist on more names.

"What about a young lady or two? You really must be considering marriage. At your age, your father and I already had two children."

The thought of an entire family dependent on him made Henry shudder. Thankfully, his mother had turned her attention to her husband and did not see it.

"What about that young lady, I believe her name is Penelope? She is Lord Johnstone's sister. How old is she?"

At the thought of courting his friend Miles's sister, Henry's eyes rounded. "I have no idea and I wouldn't dare attempt to court her. Miles has made it clear she is off limits."

"Nonsense," his mother stated.

"Besides, I have no title. I am sure they will seek a titled man for her," Henry added.

His mother rolled her eyes. "He is only speaking as a brother. Although I must admit, he has a greater understanding of your private life than we do. I hate to know why he insisted that you not court his sister."

Despite his mother's grave expression, Henry chuckled. "Mother, I am sure it is because his family has already chosen a partner for the lass. I do not know her; perhaps she is too young still for the marriage market."

"What about…?"

"I will think on it, I promise," Henry interrupted his mother. "Now tell me, who is coming to help you prepare. Alana?" he asked, knowing his mother would not wish to have his sister there at the moment. In Alana's current state of expecting her fourth child, she was a bear to be around.

It wasn't that his mother was opposed to the children, it was that his sister was rather annoying when in the family way. Complaining about everything from the weather to even the air she breathed.

Henry found it comical; his mother, not so much. The family as a whole did their best to avoid Alana, except to ensure she was well. She lived a short distance away with her ever-suffering and doting husband.

"Goodness no." His mother sipped from her cup, her eyes moving to the windows. "I have plenty of help from my friends."

IT WAS LATE in the afternoon when Henry finally left his father's study to go out. He needed to check on someone, ensure she was well.

Hannah was alone, with no family and barely enough money. Although it was not his responsibility, he'd made it so to look after her. The distraught young woman was not only reeling from her father's murder, but being abandoned suddenly by her mother, who'd decided she needed to seek solace in a convent.

That he'd been the one to find her father's body, and had given the news to both her and her mother, it set things in motion for Henry to stop by often and visit.

Hannah insisted that he should not come around and witness her mental state, but something about her pulled to him. It was more than attraction to the lovely woman. The situation brought out the protector in him; a part he'd never known before rose and demanded he ensure Hannah came to no harm.

CHAPTER TWO

HANNAH PUSHED THE curtain aside and peered out to the street. A carriage rambled by. The driver sat ramrod straight, gaze ahead. Across the street, a pair of women walked by, each with a basket hanging from their arms. In all probability, they headed to the market to shop for the day's needs. Absently, she wondered what they would purchase and if they had other problems in their life besides ensuring to prepare a good meal that day.

As of late, she'd spend most of her time indoors. Mourning her father's death meant she should not attend any social functions, nor go out to tea or other things. Not at least for a month. It had only been two weeks and already she grew restless and bored.

It would be different if she had company, but living in the house alone meant the only company was her housekeeper, Marta, who was a godsend, and a young chambermaid who came once a week to clean.

A man on horseback appeared and at once she knew who it was.

Henry Campbell.

She stared down and watched as he dismounted and tied his horse to ensure it stayed. Then straightening his jacket, he walked to the front door.

Automatically, her hand went to her hair. She'd not expected to see him that day; it had only been a pair of days since he'd last come by.

For whatever reason, Henry had taken it upon himself to be her protector and ensure all was well. As much as she looked forward to his visits, the fact that one day he would go and never return brought anxiety to her heart.

Voices downstairs told that Marta had invited him in, and Hannah glanced quickly in the mirror to see the visage of drawn features and an empty gaze. Dragging her eyes away, she exited the room and went down the stairs.

"Hello Henry," she greeted upon reaching the landing. "It is nice to see you. I did not expect your company again this week."

Butterflies tumbled in her stomach when his gaze met hers. To describe him would sound like an exaggeration. Her closest friend, Felicity Macleod, had often described him as "beautiful" and Hannah had to agree.

Henry was exquisite, there was nothing about him that was not perfect. Tall, with light brown hair that he did not have to do much to for the waves to fall into place. He had clear blue eyes that were framed by thick long lashes and further enhanced by two straight slashes for eyebrows. He had a strong jawline, and his lips were just thick enough to give a woman unseemly thoughts.

It was clear that he was either unaware of his attractiveness, or he tried his best to ignore it, not seeming to notice the looks of appreciation from both men and women whenever he entered a room.

Hannah was certainly not immune to him and had to remind herself constantly that he was only a friend, and their relationship would never go further. Not just because of the fact he'd never once attempted anything familiar, but also because their social standings were vastly different. She was on the verge of destitution and he was a member of a very wealthy family.

"Please come into the sitting room. I am craving a cup of tea." Hannah walked into the only room she and her parents had spent money on to ensure company could be hosted without showing how horrible their financial situation had become. The walls, carpets, and seating had all been updated just a pair of years past, and for it, she was glad.

Marta brought a tray with tea and two plates with a slice of cake on each. The woman was a wonder when it came to stretching the budget for food.

"What brings you today? Is there something I can help you with?" Hannah asked as she poured the tea. "I am so grateful for company. I cannot wait for another pair of weeks to pass so I can go out and do simple things." She smiled, handing Henry his cup, a tingle going up her arm when their hands touched.

"I came to see how you were. I was passing by on my way to meet with someone. Business," he clarified.

Hannah poured tea into a second cup. "I see. Well thank you so much."

"My family is hosting a party next Saturday," Henry said and visibly cringed. "Sorry. I am not sure why I am telling you as you will still be in mourning."

It was hard to not smile at his discomfort. "Even if I was not in mourning, I am sure that I would not be on the guest list. You and I are on very different social levels."

"You are my friend, and I would invite you. As a matter of fact, although you cannot attend, know that you are very much invited."

Despite the pang in her chest, Hannah chuckled. "Thank you very much, Mister Campbell. I am honored. If I were not in mourning, I would accept," she teased.

She studied him for a moment. It would make it so much easier on her foolish heart if he did not visit as often. When he married, which he would of course to a woman of his social standing, she would be devastated.

He met her gaze for a moment and then looked around the room. "Have you decided what to do about your living situation? You should not live alone."

"Says the man who is here visiting me while I am unescorted," Hannah goaded.

His sensuous lips curved, and his gaze moved to the doorway. "Your housekeeper is about."

"I have written my only aunt, who lives closer to Edinburgh, and asked if she would consider moving here to live with me. I am not sure she will agree, but she is a widow and has been alone for a few years. It could be she is ready for a change."

He nodded. "It would be a good solution. It would be safer and a way for you to continue to live in this house."

"And you should not visit as often. I know you are doing it out of kindness." She left unsaid that rumors would spread that she hosted a single man. But Hannah was not important enough for the gossips. Then again, Henry was one of the most eligible bachelors in Glasgow and he did catch the eye of the rumor mongers.

"What are your plans for the week?" he asked, sitting back, looking very much at home. For a quick moment, she pictured him living there and them having tea and discussing their weeks. It would never come to be that they would be together, but she decided to enjoy moments such as the one presently.

"I have decided to inventory all the furnishings. Those that can be repaired easily, I will see about it. Those that are no longer suitable, I will sell. Although I do not have much money to spare, I plan to redecorate the dining room and entrance. It will make me feel better. Once I am out of mourning, I can host teas and such for women friends.

"Wonderful idea," Henry exclaimed. "I will personally see to helping you get rid of the things you do not wish to keep. I know of a man who will pay for old furniture as he repairs them and sells them at a market on the outskirts of town."

Her heart warmed at how he knew people that most of his social class rarely paid any attention to. "How do you know him?"

"I have a rather large family and have helped some of my relatives with such matters." He stood, went to the doorway, and peered toward the entrance. "Once you are ready, I will personally take you to his shop. You will be amazed at his work, and I am sure you can barter with him to get replacements and repairs."

Unable to stop herself, Hannah stood and rushed to him throwing her arms around his waist and hugging him tightly. The action violated every rule of polite society, but she didn't care. "Oh Henry, thank you so much. You have no idea how much I treasure your friendship."

When she sniffed, Henry hugged her back. "Are you crying?"

"I cry about everything lately," Hannah replied, smiling up at him despite a tear trailing down her cheek. "Do not pay me any mind."

His blue gaze met hers, a soft lift to the corners of his mouth. "Of course I pay you mind." When he cleared his throat, Hannah took a step back.

"In two weeks Mister Campbell, I expect your assistance in making my house presentable for company."

When he hugged her again and pressed a kiss to her temple, Hannah let out a sigh. There was no doubt that when he married, her heart would break into a million tiny pieces.

"I best be on my way," he told her, his arms loosely around her shoulders. "Do not be sad. You can start making a list of which items you plan to do what with."

"That is a grand idea," Hannah replied with what she hoped was a brave face. "Have a good day, Henry. Thank you so much for seeing about me."

Together they went to the front door, and she stood in the doorway and watched him go to his horse and mount. Unfortunately because he donned a hat, she could not see the sunlight play on his hair. However, he cut a fine form on his horse as he waved at her and rode away.

There was something about the way he'd looked at her that was different that day. It could be her imagination, but it was as if he had a secret he wished to share but didn't dare.

"Miss Kerr, I am going to the market, do you require anything?"

Hannah turned to Marta. "I cannot think of anything. Would you please see if anyone is giving away puppies? I think I would like one for company."

"Of course." The woman went toward the parlor.

"Leave the dishes," Hannah said still looking out the window. "I will take care of it; I plan to finish my tea. Go on ahead, enjoy the pretty day."

"Very well. It would do you good to sit in the garden and get some sun," Marta replied.

Hannah nodded and smiled at the older woman. "Thank you, Marta, I will do just that."

"I HAVE BEEN knocking on the door for a long time, thank goodness it was unlocked," Felicity Macleod, her best friend, walked out to the garden and threw her wrap over a chair. "Honestly, Hannah, you should be more careful. Someone could come and accost you. You could be robbed."

"I do not have anything worth stealing," Hannah replied, standing to give her friend a hug. "I am so glad you came. Firstly, is there any news?"

Felicity sat down and gave her a worried look. "Evan went to speak to the investigator charged with your father's case," she informed her, referring to her husband.

Her stomach sunk. "And?"

"Nothing," Felicity said with a shake of her head. "No one saw anyone enter or leave the tea shop. They do not have any idea why someone would kill your father. Although the investigator did find out from a man who delivers supplies that about a month ago, a man came and argued with your father."

"Who was it?"

"The investigator would not give Evan a name. He said he

was looking for the person to speak to them."

They sat in silence for a beat while Hannah tried to gather her thoughts. "I do not know what Father got himself into, but I suspect that Mother has an idea and that is why she left."

"Why not tell you before leaving?" Felicity asked, annoyance tinging her tone. "I still am in utter disbelief that she abandoned you at such a horrible time."

"I am not sure I can ever forgive her," Hannah replied. "How could she do that to me, her only child?"

Hannah held her face up to the sky, the sun warming her skin was like a kiss. She opened her eyes and looked at Felicity. "Henry was here. Informed me his family is hosting a party next Saturday."

Her friend's brows lowered. "Why would he tell you that? You cannot be out socially."

"It was obvious after telling me, he realized his blunder. It was rather endearing that he insisted that if I were not in mourning, I was personally invited."

Felicity laughed. "He has certainly taken the role of your protector to heart. Evan commented on how he often mentions the need for you to have proper precautions in place. Being as what happened to your father and the fact you live alone."

"I am sure whatever happened that caused my father to be killed has nothing to do with me," Hannah insisted, although a shiver of apprehension traveled up her spine. "Surely they must be aware, I have absolutely no money or anything of value."

"The thought occurred to me as well. If whoever murdered your father did it because he failed to repay a loan, then it should be obvious he did not have access to any money whatsoever."

Hannah sighed. "I wish I knew what happened. It may be that I will never find out."

"I would like some tea," Felicity said, standing. "I am absolutely parched."

They went into the house through a side door that opened directly into the kitchen so that Hannah could warm water to make a pot of tea. She knew Felicity probably had errands to run and other things that were more important than spending time with her, but her friend would not leave no matter what she said.

"I brought you a few gifts," Felicity said when they went into the parlor. On a table were a few wrapped bundles, and thrown across the back of a chair, dresses and other items.

"What did you do?" Hannah asked. "Felicity, you must stop spending money on me. I can do with what I have."

"Nonsense," Felicity replied, waving off her protests. "I bought a pair of dresses and other necessary garments because once you are out of mourning, we will be going out for tea. Also I plan to host a gathering and initiate a book club. You will be helping me with it."

While Hannah opened the packages to find a silky night-gown, a pair of chemises, and some stockings, Felicity sat perched with teacup in hand looking on with the expression of a gleeful child. Her eyes twinkled and she wore a wide grin when Hannah held up the items.

She didn't have the heart to not accept them when seeing her friend beam with pride at her choices in colors and just the right touches of adornments that were exactly what Hannah would have chosen.

"I am so blessed to have you as a friend."

"You are my sister," Felicity corrected her. "And sisters take care of each other."

"Thank you. I love everything."

They spent the rest of the afternoon together. When Felicity finally left, it was almost time for supper. It was only then that Hannah realized Marta had yet to return.

She hurried into the kitchen and found it empty. Then she went through the back door and along the side of the house to peer down the street. There was no sign of Marta.

Hannah returned inside, not sure what to do. Had something happened to the woman?

By the time the sun went down, she was frantic. Just as she

was about to head to the nearest house to request that they send their coachman to ask about her housekeeper, the key in the front door stopped her.

Hannah hurried to the door to a rather frazzled Marta. The housekeeper rushed inside with a young man in tow. She slammed the door and locked it quickly.

"Miss Kerr, you are not safe. There are very dangerous-looking men asking about you."

CHAPTER THREE

After a sleepless night, Hannah got out of bed and dressed in a hurry. After Marta had told her what happened the day before, it had been impossible to sleep.

According to Marta, she'd noticed a man following her upon leaving to go to the market. It had not been much later, after she'd finished shopping, that the men approached her. A menacing-looking man had asked her if Hannah had come into a large sum of money recently. He'd insisted that Marta spy on her for him.

He'd introduced himself as a business associate of the late Mister Kerr and insisted that he'd like to hire Marta to help him collect ledgers and search for items in the house.

Marta had assured the man there was little money in the household, that the family had pinched pennies for years, and even more so now that Mister Kerr had died, along with him the income from the tea shop.

The stranger had obviously been relentless, telling Marta that there had to be money hidden somewhere. When she'd finally extricated herself from the conversation, she'd been too nervous to return to the house and instead hired a coach to take her to get someone to come and provide protection.

The ever-resourceful Marta had traveled to her village and fetched a nephew, Silas, who'd agreed to come. The young man was perhaps barely twenty, but brawny and would hopefully deter someone from approaching her.

Hannah was not sure how she would pay this nephew of Marta's. Although her housekeeper had assured her that a little something was more than he'd been making, it still bothered her.

Once on the first floor, the first thing she did was hurry to peer out the front windows. A few people were out and about, which made her feel safer. Surely no one would try to approach her in broad daylight.

"Have you considered what to do, Miss Hannah?" Marta asked, wringing her hands. "I pray someone will help." She turned to look in the direction of the kitchen. "Silas comes now."

"I do not have any idea what to do. I will visit the Murrays and ask for assistance in this."

With the young man in tow, Hannah hurried down the street in the direction of the Murrays' house. Hopefully Felicity's parents would help her.

Up until her abrupt departure, Hannah's mother and Mrs. Murray had been close friends. Mrs. Murray had been as astounded as Hannah by her mother's decision to leave so suddenly.

"You can wait for me out here," Hannah told Silas as they approached the house several minutes later. With a good-natured grin, Silas promptly sat down on the bottom step and looked up and down the street.

Hannah imagined being in the city had to be a big change for him.

"Dear one." Mrs. Murray ushered her into a beautifully furnished sitting room. "You should have sent word. I would have come to you."

Hannah hugged the woman tightly, fighting the urge to cry. The reminder of a mother figure sent her reeling. "I brought Marta's nephew, so he knows the way. In the future, he can bring notes for me."

Mrs. Murray went to the doorway and motioned to the butler. "Gerald, show the young man into the kitchen so he can have some refreshment." The woman lowered to sit and motioned for

Hannah to join her. "What happened?"

By the time Hannah finished telling her about what had occurred, she was openly weeping. Her hand shook when accepting a glass of sherry. Thankfully, the drink had the desired effect and helped settle her nerves.

"This is most dreadful. You poor dear, having to go through all this alone. I have to put my foot down and insist you come to live here, at least until you receive word from your aunt."

"I do not know what to do. I wish to move forward. I have plans to make changes to the house and sell some furniture. I want to take care of myself."

Mrs. Murray gave her an incredulous look. "What if they come to your house? They obviously think your father was hiding something."

"There is nothing of value left in the house except the pieces of jewelry Mother left, and even that would not bring enough that it was worth killing my father for."

"We will go speak to the constable," Mrs. Murray said. "If they offer protection, you must accept it. Otherwise, I will insist you come and live here."

AFTER LEAVING THE constable's station, Hannah and Mrs. Murray went to Felicity's house. It felt odd to be out after being in her house for two entire weeks. Although, if she were to be honest, Hannah cared little about social proprieties. No one other than Felicity's family and Henry had cared to check on her or see about her wellbeing after her mother left.

As far as she was concerned, she didn't owe anyone an explanation for her actions. Of course, she would not attend social functions or go to out into public places. Not because of what society expected, but because her heart was genuinely broken, and she had no desire to do much more than be alone.

Felicity's house was large and quite lovely. Along with Felicity and Evan, Grant, Felicity's brother, also lived there.

Grant was a ruggedly handsome man who was rumored to be

quite the rake, often visiting with older women who paid for his extravagant clothing and lifestyle. Yet despite his roguish reputation, Hannah liked Grant. Their families had been close since they were children.

In the parlor, they were served tea and delicious shortbread, which Hannah devoured, realizing she'd not eaten since waking.

"I can have Cook make you something more fulfilling to eat," Felicity said, a worried expression yet to leave her face. "Honestly, Hannah, I must agree with Mum, you should go live there or here. It is not safe for you to be alone."

Just then male voices carried from the entry. Three to be exact.

"Oh dear," Felicity said. "Should we tell them what happened?"

"No," Hannah said. "Henry especially. He is already going out of his way to ensure I am well. He is feeling responsible since finding my father."

"Felicity, did you hear what happened?" Evan appeared at the door, his eyes widening at seeing Hannah. "So you have."

Henry and Grant joined Evan, both looking on as Hannah blew out a breath. "I am well. There is nothing to worry about."

"We spoke to the constable, and they have agreed to send a man to walk by daily," Felicity's mother said.

"I heard about it from Marta when I stopped by to drop off sweet tarts." Henry walked into the room and met Mrs. Murray's gaze. "With all due respect to the constable and officers, once a day is not enough."

Looking up to the ceiling, Hannah could not think of what to say. Finally, she turned to Felicity. "I will stay here for the time being, but we must find out what it is those men are after. That means searching my house top to bottom."

"And finding out exactly who those men are," Grant added. "I have an idea."

Everyone turned to Grant.

His lips curved. "We will send Hannah and her housekeeper

to the market. Each of us will follow separately, at a discreet distance. When they are approached by this stranger, we attack."

"Attack?" Mrs. Murray exclaimed, her hands on her chest. "What do you mean attack?"

Felicity huffed. "Grant, you will not put Hannah in danger in that manner."

"Not to mention they could possibly be murderers," Hannah said, glaring at Grant.

"There is that," Grant admitted and sighed audibly.

The men settled into chairs and Hannah gave up trying to dissuade them. They would set a plan in motion, and she for one wanted to know exactly what they intended to do. The sooner they investigated, the sooner she would find out why people thought there was money in her house. Additionally, if they were the ones who killed her father, it could prove helpful once they informed the proper authorities.

"First things first," Evan said. "The three of us will search the house. "One of us will remain there in case one of the men come."

"I will do it," Grant and Henry said in unison.

Hannah stood. "The sooner we get this over with the better."

"First you will eat," Felicity said, leaving no room for argument. "I will check with the kitchen to make something. Let us discuss all of this over food."

Hannah was glad for the delicious meal of a simple chicken stew. While eating, everyone discussed the situation.

Despite the state of her life, one thing was certain. She was not alone; the people there in the dining room were like family. Each of them concerned for her wellbeing and doing their part to help. There was no doubt in her mind how fortunate she was.

HOURS LATER, THE search in her house continued in earnest. In her father's study, they found documentation that indicated her father had indeed sought a loan from a business called Brown Ltd. Of course, Hannah had no idea what the loan had been for.

Just after her father's murder, investigators had come and asked her mother for documents, but for some reason, she'd either not known or did not wish to provide the ones they found.

In a secret drawer of the desk, they found several hundred-pound notes. The money would be helpful, but again, not so large an amount that someone would kill over.

"I will inquire with my father about this business that Mr. Kerr had dealings with," Henry said, and looked to Grant and Evan. "You should both do the same. Perhaps one of our fathers knows them through business dealings."

Once they finished in the study, they moved to the library, which yielded nothing more than some interesting arrangement of books. Hannah had not considered it strange that her parents insisted the books be placed alphabetically by title and not by author. Apparently the norm was to place books by theme or author.

When they went to her parents' bedroom, she chose not to enter and instead went to the kitchen to seek out Marta.

The woman sat at a table with Silas, both looking glum. Marta looked up as Hannah entered. "If you go live elsewhere, does it mean you no longer require my services?" The woman wiped an errant tear.

"It is only temporary that I will be gone. I am sure this matter will be cleared up shortly. I do not wish to remain away for more than a week or two."

"So I should stay here?"

"I do not know. Would you prefer to go with me? It will be safer."

"I can take care of my aunt," Silas said. "She will be safe."

Marta nodded. "Then I prefer to remain here."

"Either Mister Murray or Campbell will be staying here to keep an eye out for anyone trying to come into the house. I feel better that you will not be alone, Marta."

When hearing the men come back down the stairs, Hannah hurried out to meet them. Henry held a box. "Does this look familiar? Do you have a key?"

It was a rather large wooden cash box and it looked heavy.

After studying the box, she shook her head. "The one from the tea shop was returned to me; you saw it in father's study. It only had a few pounds."

"We will have to force it open," Grant said. They went to the parlor where Henry placed it atop a table and then pulled a small dagger from his boot. He met her gaze for a long moment. "This may have the answers to what happened to your father."

He waited until she nodded and then made quick work of unlocking the box. The top opened upwards and in the hollow space, bundles of large notes were neatly arranged. When Henry pulled the drawer open, there were more monetary notes.

Everyone was stunned silent.

"Why have we been living in misery for years when he had all this money?"

"Perhaps he was holding it for someone," Grant mused. "Is there anything else in the box besides money?"

"No," Evan said, studying the box. "The initials atop the box do strike me as odd."

The initials "H.B." had been inscribed in an elegant font.

"I do not understand. Why is this here?" Hannah asked, knowing no one in the room knew the reply.

"My parents knew yours for a long time," Grant said. "We should ask them."

Hannah's head spun. With the amount hidden in her father's desk and the amount in the cashbox, they could have been leading a much more comfortable life. Instead, between her mother's small inheritance, and the meager profits from the tea shop, they'd barely been able to cover things like food, heating, and such.

Why had her parents hidden the money? Who did it belong to? And who was the man that appeared suddenly after his death?

CHAPTER FOUR

Henry wasn't sure what to think about the day's happenings. He entered his family home after leaving Hannah's. Grant had volunteered to spend the night there and Hannah was safe after they convinced her to stay at Evan and Felicity's for the time being.

For once, he decided to step back. There were things of his own he had to concentrate on. The amount of money required for his portion of the business deal that he'd made with his friends had to be raised. They were to sponsor a ship that was to travel to the islands and return with spices and other items that would make them very rich.

There was the matter of the ship sponsorship. His utmost concentration at the moment should be the acquisition of the capital required. He'd nowhere near the amount needed and had to figure out a way to acquire it.

At first he'd considered marriage to one of the debutants, whose families would pay a handsome dowry. But the more he considered it, the more he did not like the idea. True, his parents were anxious for him to marry. As the only son, he felt responsible to the family. Also because of his being the only son, upon his father's death, he would become wealthy and therefore was considered a great match.

However, he'd yet to regain his father's trust after the disastrous time of him losing considerable sums at the gambling dens in the city. His father had paid at first, but only to keep him alive.

Then after a stern warning, had stopped helping Henry.

Not only that, but he'd also closed his accounts and no longer provided more than a small monthly stipend and a place for him to live.

Lately, he'd acquired a bit of money from a small investment. Slowly, he'd begun to regain his father's trust and now worked alongside him and in exchange for the monthly stipend.

Henry did not begrudge his father. In his place, he too would have stopped throwing money at a son who had no regard for it.

"There you are, son," his father greeted upon his entrance. "Where have you been that you have that expression of worry?"

"More puzzled than worried," Henry said and went to the sideboard and poured brandy into a glass. "I was at the Kerrs' home..."

"Again?"

He ignored the question. "Grant, Evan and I found a box with a great deal of money. It is possible the box was the reason John Kerr was murdered." Henry took a sip, the warm liquid trailing a path down his throat. "Do you not think it is rather odd that someone would hold a large sum of money and never spend it? And go so far as to risk their life for it?"

His father, a man who loved mysteries, lowered to a chair and frowned. "Was it an old box?"

Henry described the box in great detail. "I have never seen something like it before. Quite intricately carved."

"That may be the answer." His father leaned forward in the chair, intrigued. "You must find out who made the box. Look on the bottom and see if there is an inscription."

Catriona Campbell stood at the doorway, dressed in a beautiful burgundy gown. She looked every bit the lady of the house. Her blue gaze snapped to Henry and narrowed.

"Son, we had guests for dinner. I had informed you of it and you failed to come home. I am most embarrassed and disappointed."

Another of his mother's attempts at matchmaking schemes,

he had no doubt. "I apologize, Mother, I was detained."

"There is no excuse for insulting some of the closest family friends." She swept into the room. "I took the liberty of assuring Una Stewart you would take her for a carriage ride tomorrow afternoon."

Henry suppressed the urge to groan. Not only was Una Stewart one of the most pampered and overindulged women he'd ever had the displeasure of meeting, but she was overly clingy. He'd been around her on many occasions since their mothers were friends, and always did his best to avoid being alone with her.

"I would prefer not to spend time alone with Una. She and I do not get along well."

"Nonsense," his mother replied. "She is a lovely lass, and in my opinion, a good match for you."

"I would think the lad knows who he prefers to spend time with," his father attempted to intervene. "You should not push him to a specific woman, Catriona."

His mother's right eyebrow lifted and both he and his father held their breaths.

"First of all, if I do not push this issue, we will die before our son ever marries." She gave her husband a scathing look. "Secondly, I must do everything in this matter since you, dear husband, have not made even the smallest effort to help."

When she turned to Henry, he swallowed. "You will escort Una tomorrow afternoon and ensure she has an enjoyable time."

"Additionally." She pinned him, her eyes narrowed. "You must stop this nonsense of considering yourself a champion for Hannah Kerr. I do understand you wish to be chivalrous, but you may be misleading her and giving the lass false hope. She is not an acceptable match for you, as you are well aware."

Henry exhaled. "Mother, although I have no plans to court Hannah, or anyone else for that matter, I have never considered you to be an elitist."

"I am not judging her social status as much as the fact her father had questionable connections. There are rumors all over town about why he was murdered. A man is not murdered unless there is a good reason."

His father's expression was bright when looked to Henry. "I dare say, this entire episode, as disagreeable as it is, does intrigue me. However, as you found the dead man, I think it is a good idea that you remove yourself from anything to do with it. I will look into things."

"Why?" his mother asked, shaking her head. "This has nothing to do with our family. There is no reason for us to intervene. If I were one of the investigators, I would find it strange."

"A mystery, dear, is something that has always intrigued me. There is nothing more interesting than finding out why certain things happen."

"This is a murder, William, not a game," Lady Campbell placed both hands on her hips. "I forbid any further engagement by either of you."

After a lingering murderous expression aimed at them, she turned and walked out.

"I will go and speak to the lass tomorrow," his father said with an expression of glee. "There must be something she knows that she's not said."

"Father, she's been through enough," Henry protested, once again feeling protective of Hannah. The thought of her being interrogated by his curious father made him cringe. "Mother is right, we should leave things be."

"Enjoy your carriage ride, son. One thing your mother is correct about is that you must begin the courting process. You should marry."

"Once I accomplish what I have planned and have a bank account to be proud of, I will then and only then consider marrying."

"IS IT NOT the perfect day?" Una, who clung to his arm, said the following day as they rode in a park commonly frequented for carriage rides. The canopy of trees and well-tended pathways invited the people of Glasgow to either ride the perimeter or walk on the pathways and enjoy the foliage and shade nature provided.

He studied the woman who sat across from him, Una's companion, a rather rotund woman who seemed to be constantly out of breath. The woman appeared or acted as if she was falling asleep.

From the corner of his eye, he looked to Una. "It certainly is."

Una Stewart was the middle daughter of Lord and Lady Reginal Stewart, one of four Stewart families in Glasgow. Despite the fact her father offered a generous dowry, Una had not married after her debut into society.

He would describe her as interesting in looks. Her face was triangular with a pointed chin and pursed lips. She had dark hair that was coifed into a rather complicated style. Despite attempting to smile while speaking, her expression seemed rather pinched.

With long bony fingers, she patted his leg, sending shivers up his spine. "Why were you not at dinner last night? Your mother was put out."

"I apologized profusely to my mother. Matters beyond my control kept me away until late."

There was something in her gaze, as if she tried to figure out if he told the truth, which annoyed him. Henry looked away to a passing carriage, and upon recognizing the couple, nodded in greeting.

Immediately, Una whirled to see who it was. "Was that the MacKinnons?"

"Yes," Henry replied. "Tell me, what do you spend your time doing, Una?"

At the question, Una brightened. "I am terribly busy with many things. Mother and I are patrons of the arts and theatre, and I work tirelessly to raise money for causes near and dear to my heart."

"Such as?" Henry was aware that her family often hosted formal events that were touted as fundraisers for the poor. No one had ever seen them out serving the poor, nor did they ever travel outside the circle of wealthy estates."

"The poor, of course," she replied, waving her hand. "Feeding them, clothing, things like that."

"Very admirable," he replied, to which she preened.

"Thank you."

"Do you go out personally to ensure the funds are spent well?"

"Of course not," she all but snapped. "We send people to do that. Let us speak of something brighter," she continued. "Your mother very graciously invited my family to the party next Saturday. I am very curious to know what you plan to wear. I would love to have you as an escort and wear a dress that is complementary."

"Unfortunately, I cannot escort you as Mother expects me to help host." He had to clear his throat at her presumptuous request. "Of course, I will be in attendance and look forward to seeing you there."

At being turned down, Una let out a sharp breath, then turned away and pretended to study the passing foliage.

"Who is she?"

"Excuse me?"

"There must be a woman who is taking all your attention. You have missed the last several social functions, and from what I hear, you have been busy with some mysterious cause that is causing much speculation."

Considered a popular eligible bachelor in the city, perhaps second only to Miles in desirability by mothers of elite society, he expected there to be constant rumors and gossip. Expecting it, however, did not mean it wasn't irritating.

"I have a project that I am working with three friends on. It requires a great deal of our time…unfortunately."

"If rumors are to be believed, which of course, I give them little credence..." she began then let out a huff. "Anyway, they are saying you are involved in the tea shop owner's murder."

"Thank goodness you do not give them credence, else you would find yourself in the company of a murderer this afternoon."

Una's companion gasped, her mouth opening and closing as Henry and Una looked to her, waiting to see if she could breathe. The woman swallowed. "Sir, you should not say such disturbing things."

"I apologize," Henry said, smiling at the woman, whose cheeks reddened at his attention.

Not seeming to care for attention taken from her, Una crossed her arms. "Tell me about the party? Is there a theme?"

The woman already knew. Her mother would have ensured to let her know the theme, which if he remembered correctly was garden or butterflies, or perhaps it was spring. "I do not recall the theme," he answered honestly. "As you may be aware, themes do not affect men as much as it does the lovelier sex."

Una preened at the implied compliment. "Oh I remember now. It is butterflies."

It was hard not to roll his eyes. "I am sure you will represent it perfectly."

By the time he was able to disengage from Una and ride back toward his house, Henry was much too restless to go home. "To the Macleod estate," he called out to the driver.

Upon arriving at Evan and Felicity's house, he was ushered in by the butler, who gave him a warm welcome. "Mister Campbell, everyone is in the dining room enjoying tea."

Since he'd not eaten since the morning, Henry was quite hungry. He rushed to the room, not waiting to be announced. Sometimes he forgot that Evan and Grant did not live there alone and, therefore, he had to be more mindful of social protocols.

"I am so glad to see you," Felicity said by way of greeting. It was then he noted there was no food on the table.

Instead, atop the surface, monetary notes were spread, the wooden box was open, and several pieces of parchment lay beside the items.

"What are you doing?" he asked, peering at the items.

"We are trying to solve a mystery," a booming voice replied. It was then he noticed his father was seated with a glass of what he presumed was brandy, holding a magnifying glass, inspecting a drawer from the box.

He looked to Hannah, who seemed worried, her hands gripped on her lap, rounded eyes up at him. "Your father has given us some very important information. It seems my father may have come in contact with a well-known criminal family."

At the news, he lowered to a chair, looking over his shoulder toward the kitchen. "How did you come up with that?" He met his father's bright eyes.

"The emblem on the bottom of each drawer and the box itself signified the Blackwells, a well-known crime family that embezzled money from many businesses about twenty years ago. The leader then disappeared with all the money they'd taken; neither they nor the money were ever recovered."

He met Hannah's gaze. It was evident all the talk about her father's dealings had her overwhelmed. "Would you mind a moment? I'd like a word."

She practically jumped to her feet. "Of course." They went to the kitchen, and she gave him a curious look. "Why are you coming in here?"

"I am famished," he replied, peering around for Rosalie, Evan's cook, who always ensured he was well fed.

"The servants have gone to the market," Hannah said with a soft smile. "There are scones and some sausages." She went to a covered dish and began to transfer items to a plate for him.

"You shouldn't be present during that conversation," he said, attempting to meet her gaze, which she kept lowered. "It must be horrible to hear such things."

"What is horrible..." Hannah began, "is realizing I didn't

know either of my parents at all. My father could have been involved in horrible things, and my mother, she left without a backward glance, not seeming to care that I would be left alone. She may have even been fully aware about my father's past for all I know."

"Have you considered writing her?"

"I already did. I doubt she will reply." Hannah let out a breath and attempted a soft smile. "Felicity tried to talk me out of being present during the conversation, but I insisted. I have to know."

Henry closed the distance between them and drew her into his arms. She seemed to collapse against him, to draw strength from his embrace.

His eyes closed at her body flush against his. It was much too familiar of a thing to hold a woman who was no more than a friend. And yet he felt the need to touch her each time he was near.

"Did you find what you needed?" Evan stood at the doorway.

It surprised Henry that Hannah did not jump away from him. Instead, she turned to his friend and wiped a tear. "Henry is hungry," she said by way of explanation. Then pushing the plate toward him, she went out toward the dining room.

"You made her cry?" Evan asked with an incredulous expression. "She does not need to be further distressed."

Although it was good to see that he was not the only one protective of her, Henry did not care for it. "I did not make her cry. She is upset at the situation."

"If you care for the lass, this would be the time to declare yourself. She needs someone by her side."

"I have been supportive and done all I can."

Evan gave him a knowing look. "It cannot continue, Henry. You cannot appear at her home at all hours unescorted. As much as I understand your feelings of responsibility after finding the lass's father, it is not good to give her false hope at a time like this."

"We are but friends..." he started.

"Not from where I'm standing," Evan interrupted, and then motioning to his plate, gave him a pointed look. "Come, we have some interesting developments to discuss."

Why did everyone think they could interfere in his life and give unwarranted advice?

"Bloody hell," he murmured softly and took the plate to follow Evan to the dining room.

In the parlor, his father was holding court. Explaining what he knew about the Blackwell criminals, as he put it.

Henry sat at the opposite end of the table and ate while keeping an eye on Hannah to ensure she was not overly upset by what was being discussed.

To his amazement, she held up a hand and began to talk. "I do not believe Father would have given his life to keep this money from someone. He obviously did not have plans for it as he'd never seemed to touch it. From the dust on the box, it had not been handled in a very long time." She looked to him as if seeking assurance and Henry gave a slight nod.

"What I think," Hannah continued. "Whoever approached Marta knows the money was hidden in our house, and I will gladly return it to avoid further trouble."

"Brilliant Idea," Felicity exclaimed. "Do any of you know one of those people?"

Henry and his father exchanged knowing looks. "I may know someone," Henry replied, and everyone turned to him with varied expressions of interest. He dared not meet Hannah's gaze.

"When I lost money when gambling recklessly, I owed them a large sum. Someone approached me and offered to loan me the money to cover my debts. I do not know if they were linked to the Blackwells, but it could be.

"Did you accept the loan?" Hannah asked.

Henry nodded. "I was young and stupid. I did. I was not able to pay them back as quickly as they wished. Let's just say that by the time the ordeal was over, I was beaten badly enough that my father paid the debt for fear I'd end up dead."

"It may not be the Blackwells," Evan said. "However, they may know if one of them remains in Glasgow."

With reluctance, he looked up. There was no judgment in anyone's gaze; instead, Grant slapped the tabletop. "Good, so we need you to go and speak to them."

"Wait," Hannah said, holding up both hands. "There is no need to put him or any of you in danger. If someone is to speak to them, it should be me. This is my family who is affected."

"While I admire your bravery, lass…" his father started "there is absolutely no possible circumstance in which a woman should approach any of them. Therefore, it must be a group of men, or perhaps we can send a messenger."

"Where?" Henry asked. "We cannot very well go to every gambling den and ask."

Evan spoke next. "Perhaps they will approach Marta again about returning to the market. She owes them nothing; therefore, they will not harm her. We must know who exactly knows about the box and wants it."

"The man who approached Marta did not specify a box," Hannah said. "He asked that she snoop and get ledgers and look for money."

Henry's father cleared his throat. "If they murdered your father over this, then these people or person is very dangerous."

CHAPTER FIVE

HANNAH'S TEMPLES THROBBED. The more they discovered, the more she could not believe any of the present circumstances had anything to do with her family. After asking for a few moments alone, she collapsed onto a settee in the sitting room. The room was dark as the curtains had not been pulled back that day, and it suited her perfectly.

If only she could go back in time and wake up to find she was still at home, her father alive, and all that had transpired not more than a nightmare.

However, the renewed pain behind her eyes reminded her it was all very real.

Why had her father been murdered? Killing him did not bring the murderer closer to finding the money. Had they asked him to search the house, or did he take the money and they wanted it back?

Nothing made any sense.

If only her mother had remained. Then again, it could be she didn't know anything. Or… what if she'd left because she was afraid whoever killed her father would come after her next? If that was so, she'd not cared that in leaving, Hannah was now in danger.

The entire situation left her feeling as if she never truly knew her parents. Never in the past would she have guessed that her father would be murdered over money or that her mother would have no qualms about abandoning her.

"Hannah?" Henry walked in. Each time she looked upon him, her spirits instantly lifted. Although it was unhealthy to continue the friendship, at the moment, she needed him.

One day he would walk out the door and never return. She would have to forget him. Once he married, it would be unacceptable for them to continue to be friends. As it was, they pushed the boundaries of social rules by becoming so close.

Despite what they should or should not be doing, she clung to his friendship because at the moment, he and Felicity were the only people she knew who would save her from falling into a deep pit of despair.

"Please tell me all this will all be over soon," Hannah said, looking up at him. "Say that all will be well and I have nothing to worry about."

His smile did not reach his eyes. "It will be over, hopefully soon." He sat next to her and took her hand, holding it with both of his. Strange how comfortable his closeness and touch had become. Neither of them had any qualms with touching one another. Was it because they were true friends, or because she was deeply in love with him and his spirit sensed it?

He rested on the back of the settee. "We've decided the best thing to do is to wait and see if they approach someone in the household again. If we approach the Blackwells and it isn't them who are involved, it could bring further troubles."

"I agree," Hannah said and let out a sigh. "I plan to return home tomorrow. Marta and I will be fine. There will be a constable patrolling and Marta's nephew, Silas, is staying in the house with us."

A frown marred his handsome face. "Nephew? Who is he?"

"Silas, a young man from Marta's village. Seems capable enough." Hannah sighed. "You and your father must have much to do. I beg you not to waste any more time on this."

They sat in silence for a long spell.

"I do have to prepare for the party."

Henry's tone made her chuckle.

"I am sure you will have a delightful time. Felicity is looking forward to it."

"Will you come?" he asked, turning to her. "You do not have to dance, you can just be company for Felicity."

"No," Hannah replied, her chest constricting. "I am still in mourning. Besides, I am sure your mother would be put out that you invite a single woman to what, I am sure, is an occasion to help find your future wife."

"My coming out ball," Henry said and held up a hand, with his pinky out. "Oh dear, what should I wear?"

Hannah laughed despite the tangible pain that racked through her heart. "I am sure you will look perfect. Every eye will be on you."

This time he chuckled. "When I marry, it will be the woman of my choice, not someone handpicked by my mother because of what she and Father consider a good match."

"I have no doubt you will find the perfect woman." Hannah pulled her hand free of his when she heard footsteps.

Felicity hurried into the room, her eyes bright. "What are you two discussing?"

"Henry's coming out ball," Hannah replied with a smile.

"Oh yes," Felicity said, lowering to a chair opposite them. "It is the talk of the town. The butterfly event at the Campbell estate."

"Butterflies?" Hannah wondered what the significance was.

"Mother's idea," he replied. "She loves the creatures."

"Butterflies are beautiful," Felicity said. "I am wearing several in my hair. I am also having the seamstress embroider one into the bodice of my gown."

Hannah nodded, feeling left out, but in a way, she was used to not being part of her best friend's social circles. "I hope to see you in it."

"I must bid you both goodnight," Henry said, standing. "I must rescue Evan and Grant from my father."

When he placed a kiss to her temple, Hannah's eyes rounded.

When they were alone, it didn't matter, but that he did so in front of Felicity made her uncomfortable.

"All will be well. You will see," he said, and to her consternation, took her hand and squeezed it.

He nodded at Felicity and walked out.

"Before you say anything, I do not know what came over him to take such liberties." Hannah didn't dare look at Felicity directly.

"The man is madly in love with you and has yet to admit it to himself." Felicity beamed at her. "I believe the feeling is mutual."

Hannah shook her head. "Whether I have feelings for him or not does not matter. He will marry the daughter of a lord, or a duke. Not a woman who lives alone and whose father was murdered, and mother absconded."

"You do have a very sordid life, Hannah. When this is all over, you should write a book." Only Felicity could turn things to a place no one would think about.

"When this is over, I plan to continue with my plans to redecorate my house one room at a time until it is beautiful, and I can host teas and perhaps this book club of yours."

"That is boring," Felicity said. "What if we go on a trip? Or perhaps plan a summer masquerade party?"

Hannah met her friend's gaze. "Here at your house. No one will come to my house. There are too many shadows in the corners."

That night as she lay in bed and considered the events of the day, the thing that stood out the most was how kind Henry's father had been. Upon entering, he'd asked to be introduced to her and had ensured Hannah no harm would come to her.

He'd also insisted on being included in helping. According to Henry, his father was a keen investigator by nature and had often assisted the local constable with cases that were hard to solve. Having the gentleman of such high standing included hopefully meant that things would be resolved soon.

There was the situation with Henry that she refused to face.

She would have to prepare her heart for the fact that he would be marrying. That was the reason for the party after all. To ensure Henry met eligible women.

Despite Felicity's opinion, that they had strong feelings for one another, Henry would one day inherit his father's vast fortune. And because of it, he had a responsibility to his family.

He had to marry a woman of his social standing, not one who was not only beneath him socially, but brought with her the scandal of murder.

WALKING TO THE market with Marta had been Hannah's idea. She'd not cleared it with any of the people at Felicity's house. It was Saturday, the day of the Campbell party, and she needed the distraction of being outdoors. Besides, nothing was more distracting than the possibility of being approached by a killer.

She and Marta lingered in front of several stands, purchasing bread, meat, and vegetables. No one paid either of them any mind, perhaps because Marta's nephew stood a short distance away.

"I see him," Marta whispered.

Hannah's heart jumped in her chest. "Where?"

"What do you think?" Marta said loudly, holding up a bunch of carrots, and then lowered her voice. "Look past the carrots to the man leaning on the tree."

Holding out her hand to touch the carrots, Hannah saw the man. He was bulky, whether from muscles or fat, it was hard to tell since he wore a long black coat.

"Are you sure?" Hannah said, putting the carrots into her basket.

"A pence," the woman at the stall called out.

Marta paid the woman and they moved to the next stall. "What should we do?"

"I have no idea," Hannah said. "I wish I could see his face clearly."

They walked to where a man sold chickens and Hannah asked for one. The bird was quickly killed, tied together, and handed to Marta.

The entire time the man watched from a distance. He'd moved to keep up with them, not bothering to keep from being noticed. He wanted Marta to see him.

"We should not have come alone," Marta said, shivering. She motioned to Silas. "Stay close."

Hannah had to admit, it was unsettling to be watched by someone who could possibly mean them harm. She searched the area for a constable, but there were none to be found.

Just then she spotted one. With the ease of a man of authority, the officer swung his club and walked assuredly down the street.

"I should speak to him." Hannah hurried toward the officer, who noticed her and stopped walking.

"Is everything all right, Miss?" he asked, glancing around. Upon spotting the man in the black coat, his eyes narrowed.

Obviously the man had a reputation. The man in the black coat began to whistle and strolled away.

"He kept watching us," Hannah told the officer. "Do you know who he is?"

"A petty thief. Often paid to do things such as watch people and collect debts. I would return home and ensure next time to be in the company of your husband. If someone in your household has debts with people of dubious nature, they should pay."

"I do not have any dealings with anyone of any bad reputation. I live with my maid. There was no reason for that man to watch me."

The constable did not seem overly worried about her safety. "His street name is Beans. I would keep my distance."

"Aren't you going to go after him?"

"Miss, there is no law against looking at someone."

Annoyed, Hannah began to walk in the direction the man—Beans—went. The constable hurried alongside. "What are you doing, Miss?"

"I am going to ask him what he wants and why he approached my housekeeper last week."

"You didn't tell me about that." The officer sounded winded.

Noting that the man had stopped, and did not notice they walked towards him, she hurried her pace. "I made a report."

"Miss, you should stop at once," the constable managed to say just as they reached the man, who turned and looked at them wide-eyed.

Hannah stepped up to the man, who was shorter than she expected. "Sir, you approached my housekeeper last week and now, today, you followed us."

"I 'ave no idea what this woman is talking about," the man sputtered, looking from her to the constable. "A man can look and be to 'imself."

The constable seemed to regain his composure. "Beans, did you approach the lady's housekeeper?" At this point, Marta and Silas had caught up.

Hannah motioned to Marta. "Tell the constable what I say is true."

Marta nodded, her eyes moving from Beans to the officer. "He asked me to steal ledgers from the house."

"I see." The constable turned to Beans, who began walking backwards.

"I did nothin'." Beans turned on his heel and ran. The constable chased him, blowing a whistle to alert others if they were near.

Hannah, Marta, and Silas stood in a line watching as Beans did his best to run, but he was not very fast. The constable seemed to be losing his breath too, his face turning red.

"I better help." Silas took off sprinting across the market, cutting through the middle. Within moments, he caught up to Beans and tackled him to the ground.

"Ha!" Marta exclaimed. "That's why it's better to raise lads in the country. Lots of room to run."

Hannah began to shake as they watched the constable and another one who'd materialized drag Beans off. "I suppose we will have to go to the constable's offices to see what they find out."

"Perhaps you should get someone to go with you," Marta said. "I do not think a young lass should go there without escort."

"You're correct," Hannah said. "Everyone is attending the party. I am not sure who to ask."

"What about Mister Murray?"

"They are going to the party as well." They began walking home. "You and Silas could go with me. I will hire a carriage."

Just then Silas caught up. The young man was barely out of breath, and he beamed with pride. "The constable said you need to stop by the station, Aunt Marta."

"When?" Marta asked. "I have chores."

"Once we put the purchases away, we will all go," Hannah said. "We must find out what he knows and then hopefully I will get closer to finding the truth about my parents and what secrets they held."

By the time they arrived at the constable's office, there wasn't anything new to learn. It turned out Beans refused to talk. He was held only for a couple hours, which in Hannah's opinion, didn't last long enough.

"What can we do now?" Marta asked as they arrived back at the house.

Hannah felt as if she'd been kicked in the stomach. "We will wait. If he is being paid to find out information, then he will not stop. Ensure you take Silas with you when going to the market."

Upon entering her bedroom, the room was cool, but she didn't mind. Hannah fell back on the bed and closed her eyes. Everyone was at the Campbells' tonight. She imagined the bright ballroom, music filling the air and people dancing. There were probably many single women there, as the event was at Henry's home.

Was he enjoying being the center of attention, or bothered? Hannah smiled. In most likelihood, he was annoyed. Then again, if a certain young lass caught his attention, he was having a good time.

Her chest constricted at the thought. Why did she have to fall in love with someone out of reach?

The question was ridiculous. Henry Campbell was so very kind to her. There was something about him that made her feel different. When he was near, the air was lighter, and everything seemed to fall into place. And his touch, although she was sure it was meant as only friendly, made her feel as if she could face down the world.

Blowing out a breath, she went to the window and caught a glimpse of two constables speaking. They seemed relaxed, one smoking, the other pointing in the direction of her house as they spoke. It was reassuring that they were indeed patrolling nearby.

Still, there had to be something more that could be done. Someone wanted her father's ledgers and the money. But who?

Perhaps it was time to visit her mother and find out the extent of what she knew. Her aunt had yet to reply to the letter, which did not bode well.

No matter. She would ask Felicity to accompany her to the convent as soon as possible. Whether or not her mother wished to speak to her didn't matter. Hannah would give her no choice in the matter.

WITH EVAN FOR company, Hannah and Felicity left for the convent early that morning. The carriage rolled over an uneven road heading toward the village where Hannah's mother had gone. The convent was housed in a rather odd building. It was as if it was built haphazardly, rooms added on as needed.

As the carriage continued toward the front of the building, several nuns, bent over in gardens, straightened and looked on with curiosity as they rode past.

Barely able to breathe past the constriction in her chest, Hannah managed to climb out of the carriage, her hands shaking. After the heartless way her mother had left, with scarcely any kind of explanation other than following her true calling, Hannah had absolutely no desire to see her.

"Perhaps we should wait a bit," Felicity said, placing a hand on Hannah's shoulder. "You look pale."

She met her friend's gaze. "I must speak to her. I fear my reaction upon seeing her. I did not wish to ever speak to her again. But I must."

Felicity nodded in understanding. "I will not leave your side. I promise." Her dear friend clutched her hand. "Let us see what she has to say."

"I will wait here," Evan stated, although it was redundant as men would not be allowed inside.

The mother superior was less than pleased at their presence. "When Sister Margaret arrived, she left all behind. You must understand, I cannot allow a visit."

"Sister Margaret? How refreshing to be able to escape and start anew," Hannah replied in a bitter tone. The last word caught in her throat, she closed her eyes and stopped speaking.

Thankfully, Felicity would not allow them to fail. "She left my friend, her daughter, behind, not only without chaperone or protection, but right after her father was murdered. Now, whoever murdered her father is now threatening Hannah. *Sister* Margaret will either speak to us, or I will ensure the authorities visit next." Felicity's tone was sharp, her words without inflection except when stating the word "sister."

The nun faltered, her gaze pinning Felicity before looking to Hannah, who at this point was seething.

"Why is it that she gets to abandon her responsibilities? Fleeing whatever threatens and finds protection. I understand this is a new life for her, Mother Superior, but she must help me. She is still my mother."

"This is a matter of life and death," Felicity added. "We must speak to her."

After a few moments of the woman seeming to calculate what was best to do, she finally relented. "Very well. Wait here."

"The audacity of that woman acting as if we are the ones in the wrong." Felicity paced, obviously as angry as Hannah.

"If the situation was different, we would be," Hannah replied, attempting to calm her racing pulse. "If she doesn't know anything, then her only crime is leaving me behind."

When the door opened and a woman walked in, Hannah fought to recognize the woman who entered. Her mother seemed to have aged ten years, her face drawn. Upon seeing her, she turned back to the door as if about to flee.

"Do not run away again," Hannah said, barely recognizing the steel in her own voice. "Once you answer my questions, you can go back to your new life and never see me again."

Dressed in novice clothing, her mother collapsed into a chair, her gaze never meeting Hannah's or Felicity's. "What is it?"

When Felicity started to say something, Hannah stopped her.

"A man has confronted Marta and followed me. He asked Marta to fetch Father's ledgers and find money that is hidden in the house. I have to live in fear with constables patrolling the house."

Her mother's eyes snapped to her and then quickly away, confirming she did know something.

"You must tell me what you know. They are threatening me." Hannah fought against shaking the woman.

"Threatening?" It was as if she was talking to herself, not looking at anyone. "Why would they threaten you? You do not know anything."

"Who are they?" Felicity asked. "You must tell us."

A tear rolled down Margaret's hollow cheek. "I left in hopes they would give up. I did not want any of this to happen."

Hannah and Felicity exchanged looks. Neither wanting to interrupt, they remained silent.

"It is all my fault. I failed your father. I failed God."

That she didn't mention failing her, made Hannah grit her teeth, but she remained silent.

The story tumbled out, in disjointed bits and pieces, none of it making sense.

"I was already with child when I met your father. We agreed to keep it a secret. My son. I said he was dead. But the father never stopped blaming me. He thought I killed the babe. I took the box of money from him and escaped."

By the empty look on her mother's face, she was not there in the room, but transported to the past.

"When he found me again, I was going to leave, to come here and answer my true calling. But then you." Her gaze was accusing when finally meeting Hannah's. "I was with child again."

"What does the man want?" Hannah asked softly.

"He is the one who burned down our business. Probably who killed John. I cannot prove it, but I am sure it was him. I could not give him anything. I do not know where the money is. I'd asked the housekeeper who worked with us before Marta to hide it well."

"Why didn't you return it to him?" Felicity answered.

"She died suddenly. I searched and searched, but never found it."

"Who is he?" Hannah asked again. "You must tell me. Who is the man you had a child with?"

CHAPTER SIX

"THE EVENING WAS a success," his mother announced at breakfast that morning, her face alight with happiness.

Henry's heart softened; it was always nice to see her happy. "Yes it was, Mother. You outdid yourself. Everyone commented on the beautiful décor."

"There are butterflies everywhere," his mother commented with a smile. "I hope they make their way to the garden."

The night before, living butterflies had been released just outside the doorways. Unfortunately, lured by the light, many had instantly flown into the ballroom. Many had fluttered about the room, landing wherever they wished, unfortunate ones straight into candle flames.

It had been a bit comical, as some of the ladies did not care for them sitting in their hair adornments. Everything had settled when the musicians played a lively waltz, luring the guests back to the dancing.

"Where is Father?" Henry asked.

"He is unwell this morning. Imbibed a bit too much last night," his mother replied with an annoyed expression.

THE GENTLEMAN'S CLUB was emptier than usual when he arrived. Henry assumed it was because most of the usual patrons had been at his house the night before.

Upon spotting Lord Miles Johnstone, Henry went to sit in a chair next to the brooding man.

A server immediately materialized, and although Henry was not in the mood to imbibe, he ordered whiskey.

"What has you in a dour mood this morning, friend?" he asked Miles, who nodded by way of greeting.

"My plans have been thwarted and I am not pleased," Miles replied. "I've wasted weeks only to be turned away."

Henry let out a bark of laughter. "You, Lord Johnstone, the most eligible bachelor in Glasgow has not gotten his way? We have wondered where you had been as you've been scarcely seen about town."

"Paris," Miles replied, the word dripping with annoyance. "I've been in Paris."

"I hear the food is good," Henry replied, accepting the glass of amber liquid. "What happened?"

"She wanted marriage."

"Ah."

"So without a proposal, no money."

Miles shrugged. It was obvious he was not heartbroken. It was more his pride, as he'd expected his company and attention alone should have lured the woman to hand over a huge amount of money. To Miles, the entire thing was more of a game, a competition. If his friends could come up with the sum needed for the investment through seduction and prowess, he wished to do the same and perhaps even better in some way.

The only reason Henry found the entire thing amusing was because Miles did not need the money. He was wealthy and had more than enough to fund his portion without help.

"So we are both in the same situation," Henry said. "I have yet to find the woman who will help me. Last night at the ball, there was one who had promise. But for some reason, I cannot do it. I cannot make myself seduce someone right now."

"There is only one reason for that," Miles said with a pointed look. "You are in love with someone else. Perhaps someone who cannot give you the money."

At the words, Henry started to adamantly deny it, but the rebuttal stuck in his throat. Was he in love? Or just infatuated?

Hannah Kerr was indeed in his thoughts constantly and there was nothing he enjoyed more than being in her company. However, the fact he liked to be with her did not make it love.

"I am not in love."

Miles did not reply. The man had a way of looking at a person and seeming to see past all pretenses. Most of the time, Henry found it amusing. This day, however, he did not.

"What? Why are you looking at me that way?"

"Is it that what started out as feeling responsible for Miss Kerr has turned into something deeper? You do not know it yet perhaps, how deep your feelings go." Miles had the nerve to smile.

"What is your plan now?" Henry asked, purposely changing the subject. "Knowing you, there is already something in the works."

"A woman by the name of Louisa Kent has arrived in Glasgow. She purchased a large home not too far from Evan and Felicity. I am sure our dear friends will not hesitate to have her for tea."

"And you, being a thoughtful gentleman, will not only be at this tea, but you will insist on showing her around Glasgow."

Mile's lips curved. "Of course."

The plan had promise and Henry wondered if he could perhaps intercede and beat Miles to the woman.

"Luckily, Grant has left to the continent. He is traveling with the woman who he expects will give him all the money he requires."

"If his plan does not work, he will be hard-pressed to come up with the money in a very short time."

Henry chuckled. "I am confident in our friend. He will have the money."

"What about you?" Miles asked, his gaze once again delving. "What is your plan?"

"I am going to ask my father for a loan."

It was an hour or so later that they walked out. Miles looked to Henry. "Where are you going?"

"To see Evan."

"He is not home. I went over there earlier, and George informed me they'd gone to the convent to see Hannah's mother."

The news struck him oddly. In that moment, he felt left out of something important. "How far is it?"

Miles shrugged. "I am not sure, half a day, maybe further. I would be surprised if they return today."

Looking on as his friend mounted and tapped his hat in farewell, Henry remained rooted to the spot. Why had they decided to go to the convent? Something must have happened the day before.

He mounted and guided his horse to Hannah's house.

The housekeeper did not seem surprised to see him. Since he often visited, the woman was used to his unannounced visits.

"I hear Hannah went to see her mother," Henry started as he walked into the foyer. "What happened?"

Marta motioned him to the sitting room. "Would you like to sit down, Mister Campbell?"

"No, thank you," Henry replied, trying to keep from sounding impatient. "I am not staying."

The housekeeper seemed to consider whether to reply or not. "The man who approached me the other day at the market. Miss Hannah and I saw him yesterday. He was arrested but refused to talk. Miss Hannah decided to seek answers from Missus Kerr."

"Did the man try to approach you? Who is he?"

"He did not, especially when Miss Hannah went to a constable. They chased him and my nephew Silas caught him. He is a man called Beans. I do not know his first name, but his last name is McBean."

Henry nodded. "Thank you."

Moments later, he rode near the market and slowed his mount. At a leisurely pace, he continued past the stalls of fruits and wares until spotting the man in question. He knew him. Years ago when pursued for payment of his debts, this particular man had been sent to find him.

Although the man had not caught him—Henry was a fast runner—he remembered Beans clearly.

Henry dismounted and walked closer until catching the man's gaze. "It has been a long time since you've chased me," Henry said by way of greeting.

Beans' yellowed gaze narrowed. "If I were you, I would keep walking."

"Who do you work for now? The Blackwells?"

At the mention of the name, Beans looked around. "Go away. Yer fancy clothes will not stop me from punching you."

The man seemed to lose some bravado when Henry walked closer and squared his shoulders. He was almost a foot taller than when the man had chased him. "Who hired you to follow Hannah Kerr? That is all I want to know."

The man let out a dry bark of laughter. "You and everyone else. If I talk, I will ruin my reputation."

"I think you will give me a hint for coin." Henry pulled notes from his pocket and glanced down as if noticing them for the first time. "Who?"

Beans looked around, scanning the area. "You do not know him. Brown. Jules Brown." Beans snatched the money and hurried away. Apparently, this Jules Brown did not pay much.

With his newly acquired information, Henry wasted no time. He went to the one place where he could find anyone. One of the few places in Glasgow where information about who was who flowed freely.

The women of his mother's quilting group looked up and beamed at his entrance. Lady Campbell, not so much. Her eyes narrowed with suspicion. "What brings you, son?"

After greeting the five women in the room, he went to his

mother and kissed her temple. "I am searching for Father, but upon seeing you and your friends, I wished to greet everyone."

"How polite," his mother replied dryly. "I wished to speak to you this morning after breakfast, but you went out."

Henry nodded. "I had a business meeting with Miles. After I rode past the market." He produced a beautifully embroidered handkerchief. "I got this for you."

"Thank you." His mother, who loved getting gifts, smiled.

"Mother, have you heard of someone named Jules Brown? Are there any people that we know with that last name?"

His mother shook her head. "Not that I can recall."

"I knew someone named Brown," one of the women said, Lady Wilshire, one of the town's biggest gossips. "A rather interesting man," she began, getting everyone's attention. "You must remember him, ladies. He was the one who owned the building before the Kerrs did. The one that burned."

Henry's gut clenched. "Where is he now?"

Mrs. Wilshire waved her hand dismissively. "He died not long ago. I believe from illness."

Another woman nodded enthusiastically. "That's right, I remember now. I believe his name was Horace Brown. He was well known for being eccentric."

"I had no desire to get to know that man, always made me uncomfortable," Lady Wilshire stated with a shudder.

The women began to discuss the different illnesses that could claim a man and Henry made his way back to the door. His mother's questioning gaze met his just as he walked out.

Everything was falling into place, and yet so many questions remained. The following day, he would visit Hannah. Hopefully she gathered information from her mother that would help them figure out what threatened her.

HIS FATHER FINALLY appeared at dinner, looking well-rested. He met Henry's gaze. "Did you meet with the actuary today?"

"Yes Father, I did. All is in order. He left some documents for you to sign," Henry replied.

"It is good to see you two working together," his mother added. "I do have a question for you, dear." She looked to Henry. "Why were you asking about a man called Jules Brown?"

At the mention of the name, his father straightened. "I recall that name. Not sure from where."

It was best to tell them, despite knowing they, especially his mother, would object to him being so focused on a situation that had nothing to do with the family.

"The man who approached Hannah Kerr's housekeeper is a street runner called Beans. I saw him today and questioned him. With reluctance, he admitted to being hired by a man called Jules Brown."

At the information, his father stopped eating and leaned forward, his eyes wide with anticipation. "Is that so. Jules, is he related to Horace Brown?"

"I do not know." Henry continued doing his best to ignore his mother's irritated expression. "However, this Horace Brown owned the building before John Kerr acquired it."

He almost smiled when his father rubbed his hands together with glee. "It must all be connected. The burning of the building, the money box and the murder."

"For goodness sakes," his mother exclaimed. "This is not a topic for a dinner conversation."

"Do you not see how very interesting this all is?" his father asked.

As expected, his mother gave them each a pointed look before stating the obvious. "This has nothing to do with our family. Delving into matters such as this can be dangerous. Do you wish for harm to come to us? Some things are best left to the authorities."

"I am only providing assistance by studying the facts," his

father replied, his tone filled with pride. "They very much need the opinion of an expert in rational studies."

Henry looked at his plate to keep from chuckling.

"And you?" his mother asked. "What exactly is your interest in this?"

For a moment, Henry had to ask himself the same question. Why was he so invested?

"Hannah is my friend. I found her father..."

His mother held up a hand to stop him from speaking. "That does not make you responsible for the lass. She has the support of the Murrays and the MacLeods. It is much more than people of her social standing could ever hope for."

He bit back the annoyance he felt at his mother's estimation of Hannah.

"She is a good person, Mother. I admire her greatly."

"Do not allow this admiration to be more than that. You are not about to ruin everything by setting your sights on someone who is not of our social class."

His mother was a kind person who worked tirelessly to help the impoverished in the city. And yet did she ever really notice them?

"I find it hard to reconcile your works for the needy with your predisposition against those that have less than us."

Lady Campbell sighed and shook her head. "I have higher aspirations for you son, that is all."

CHAPTER SEVEN

HANNAH DOUBLECHECKED TO ensure all the doors and windows were locked despite the fact Marta had insisted they were. Silas slept on the first floor in a small room beside her father's study that they'd emptied. The fact the young man was in the house along with Marta, who'd moved into Hannah's old bedroom, made her feel safer.

Both Marta and Silas had gone to bed and the house was quiet. Hannah could not fathom sleeping. Instead, she paced in the parlor, attempting to gather her whirling thoughts into some sort of cohesion.

She'd asked to return home after leaving the convent. More than anything because every inch of the house needed to be searched.

Hannah wanted to make sure there weren't any other secrets hidden.

Her mother had given her very little information, refusing to name who she'd stolen the money from. It was obvious, to Hannah at least, that her mother was not in her right mind."

When Mother Superior returned to inform them they had to leave, Hannah had pulled the woman aside and explained how she felt about her mother's mental state.

In that moment, it was obvious the nun expected as much. She promised to keep her apprised if anything happened.

A soft rapping at the glass made her freeze and Hannah considered calling for Silas. Because there were several lanterns in the room, it made it hard to see out. But she noted the outline of a man and wondered if it was one of the constables.

Narrowing her eyes, she went closer, prepared to call to Silas if it was someone who meant harm.

"Henry?" She opened the French doors to allow him in. "What are you doing here so late? It is dangerous to be out."

He walked in and removed his hat but left the caped overcoat on. "I must speak to you."

They stood still for a long moment, the silence enveloping them whirling around, a silent mist of questions and expectations.

At once all the burdens of the day overcame her and Hannah fell against his chest, the cold outer garment sending shivers through her. "I am glad you are here."

His hat hit the floor with a soft thud.

When she looked up, he kissed her. The softness of the kiss brought tears to her eyes. She clung to him, needing to be close, and prayed he did not pull away.

A wave of relief fell over her when he wrapped his arms around her and deepened the kiss, his mouth pressing against hers in a manner she never expected. Then his tongue pressed against the seam of her lips, and she parted them to allow it past.

Every sensation pulsed through her body when he tipped her face up so that he could continue exploring her mouth with his.

Although a novice and not having been so thoroughly kissed before, Hannah responded. Raking her fingers through Henry's hair and pressing her body against him did not sate the need that suddenly burned.

When tingles of heat traveled through her body to the most intimate of places, Hannah pushed away abruptly.

"Ah. I-I think we should not," Hannah stuttered, her eyes glued to his. "Why are you here?"

His chest lifted and lowered as Henry fought to catch his breath. Hannah wondered if he'd felt something similar. Surely not. After all, she had no doubt he'd kissed other women and was a great deal more experienced than she.

Instead of answering, he bent to pick up his hat and placed it on a table, then he removed his coat and carefully folded it over a chair.

There was a softness in his eyes when he looked at her. "I needed to see you after hearing where you went. Are you well?"

"Yes. I am a bit overwhelmed."

"Please sit." He motioned to the settee. "I found out something today."

"Would you like some tea?" Hannah replied, thinking it was best to leave the parlor and go to a less secluded room. Then again, they were alone in a practically empty house.

"If you wish," he replied, following her out of the room. Just as they walked out, Silas appeared in the doorway.

"Is everything in order, Miss Hannah?" His sleepy gaze moved to Henry.

Hannah nodded. "All is well. Go back to sleep."

Once in the kitchen, Hannah put the tea kettle on to heat. "I will hear about this from Marta tomorrow."

"I would not come so late, but this is important."

"Miss?" Marta appeared. "What happened?"

Henry motioned to the housekeeper. "Please sit, you have to hear this as well."

The women exchanged looks and Marta sat. "Bad news?"

"No," Henry replied. "I found the man Beans. He informed me that he was paid by a man called Jules Brown. Do either of you know this man?"

Both shook their heads, gazes glued to Henry.

"Father and I believe this man Jules is the son of Horace Brown. I found out that Horace used to own the building that your father owned, the one that burned."

"Goodness, what is happening?" Hannah said. "I do not understand."

"I spoke to one of the men who investigated the fire before coming here," Henry continued. "Rumors ran during the time of the fire that Horace had burned the building. However, it could not be proven. The investigator told me they could not figure out why, but they were certain Horace had a grudge against your father."

Henry met Hannah's gaze. "Horace Brown died recently from illness."

"My God," Marta said crossing herself. "This is like a bad dream."

"I may know why," Hannah replied. "It is making more sense."

Marta hurried to the teakettle and poured the hot liquid into three cups. Then, looking to the doorway, poured a forth. Silas walked in and sat down.

Hannah let out a long breath. "I found out today that Mother was with child upon meeting my father. The father of her child demanded to know what she'd done with the boy. She told him the boy was dead. According to Mother, she took the box of money and came here to Glasgow to hide."

"What of the babe?" Marta asked.

"All she said was that she told the man he was dead. However, she did not say he'd actually died. She was not in her right mind. It was obvious this entire sequence of events unsettled her greatly."

"Jules may be that boy, must want the money," Silas finally spoke. "Do you think he is your half-brother?"

Hannah shook her head. "I do not know. It could be that somehow Horace found him and told him everything before dying."

"I will find this Jules, and when I do, you and I can go speak to him." Henry stood. "I apologize again for the late hour. I felt that you should know this information as soon as possible."

"Thank you," Hannah replied. "I will walk you to the door." She returned to the kitchen where Marta and Silas continued to sit. "What do you think, Marta?" Hannah asked. "Did you ever hear of Jules Brown before?"

The housekeeper shook her head. "Once I did hear your

parents in a heated conversation. Your father insisted she tell him about a boy. It did not make sense at the moment, but now, I wonder if they spoke about the babe."

"They kept many secrets," Hannah said quietly. "Too many secrets."

⋙⋘

"WHILE STARTING ON my plans to redecorate the house, it will give me the opportunity to search for any other items that may help us discover what is happening," Hannah explained to Felicity and her mother, who'd stopped by the following afternoon.

All the furniture from the dining room had been dragged into the hallway and sitting room so that the walls and carpet could be redone.

Amidst the flurry of activity, she'd forgotten that the ladies were to stop by to discuss the ongoing issue of the money box.

"After much discussion with Evan, we think it is best to disclose the box and its contents to the constable. That way it is reported and confirmed as your property. Anyone wishing to snatch it is then a thief," Felicity said.

"My husband agrees," Felicity's mother added.

Marta brought tea and they were silent as Hannah poured.

"It is a good idea," Hannah replied. "However, for one day, or two, I would like to not think about that odious object."

"What about the money?" Felicity pointed out. "You need it, Hannah. It will ensure you are secure and can provide for yourself well. Although admittedly, you still require a chaperone or a better living arrangement than the present."

"Marta is my chaperone. I have not heard from my aunt. Which, her being my mother's sister does not surprise me. It is obvious they are selfish people."

"I am so sorry." Felicity reached out, placing her hand on Hannah's forearm.

Felicity's mother sighed. "I would have never thought Margaret would be so heartless. How could she just leave?"

"Oh if you would have seen her, Missus Murray, you would have understood. She is not well mentally."

Her friend gave her a bright smile. "Evan and Henry have hired a private investigator to find this Jules Brown and what he is about. They'd planned to find him themselves until I threatened to call the constable."

"Always the heroes," Hannah said with a smile. "I appreciate everything. All of you have replaced the family I have lost."

Poor Silas was exhausted by the time the ladies left. Each of them had ideas as to what furniture should be placed where.

The sideboard from the dining room was moved to the entryway, as well as a rug that had not been used in a long time.

Hannah polished the piece and then placed a large vase that was also from the dining room atop it. Immediately, the area was transformed beautifully, and she took a step back to admire the work.

"Missus Murray has a good eye for décor," Marta said, coming up behind her. "Eileen is here to help clean. I will take advantage of her keeping you company, Miss Hannah, and go visit my sister."

"Yes, please go," Hannah replied while adjusting a picture on the wall. "I will be fine. Please take Silas so that you are safe just in case."

Hannah walked into the empty dining room, and unable to do much in there, found herself ambling into her father's office.

With the housekeeper in the parlor, she decided it was as good a time as any to begin searching for more information.

First she sat in the chair behind the desk and placed her hands flat on the surface. "What other secrets did you have, Father? Why were you murdered?" Her gaze moved over the familiar surface. On the desk was an inkwell and quill. A lantern, wax, and seal along with small stacks of invoices and notes.

Her father took advantage of every scrap of paper to scribble notes that made no sense to anyone but him. Reminders of deliveries, of items to order, even who was owed what.

The corner of a page stuck out from one of the ledgers and she pulled it out. It was another of his notes that listed items. Milk, black tea, sugar, cinnamon, nutmeg. Nothing unusual, except it was strange that he would list such basic ingredients. He must have been considering a blend of coffee perhaps. At the bottom of the paper, the words caught her attention.

Margaret must know. Ask again.

Her poor father. Was he trying to goad his wife into telling him where the box of money was? It was possible he was receiving threats on his life and the only way to save himself would be to find the money.

Then again, if he had no idea where the money was, or if it even existed, then he could not very well find it.

Why hadn't her mother torn the house apart to find it? In the end, it had not been too hard to find the loose floorboard and, in turn, the box.

Hannah placed the note atop the ledger and stood. She walked to a shelf and began pulling books in order to look behind them.

By the time she was finished searching the bookshelves, the sun was setting. Other than the note, she'd found nothing of interest.

"That is because you did not know anything," she murmured. "Mother was who kept the secrets."

It was a good thing her mother was closeted far from there and in a convent because Hannah would not have been able to control her reaction if she saw her. How could the woman stand by while her husband asked about the money?

A tear trailed down her cheek at the thought of her father's last moments. He must have been so afraid.

Footsteps sounded and Hannah wondered if Eileen was leaving.

"Eileen? Have you finished?" Hannah asked, walking out of the study. There was only silence.

"Marta?"

Again, no reply. Sure she'd heard footsteps, she inched back into the study and scanned the room for something she could use as a weapon.

CHAPTER EIGHT

IF NOT FOR the fact that Evan and Miles were also in attendance, at yet another social function, Henry would have left. He'd wanted to stop by and see Hannah, however, he'd been detained until late at a business meeting.

"Is she the lucky woman to be on your arm for the rest of the Season?" Miles asked, his gaze moving across the room to where Una stood next to his mother.

"I hope not," Henry replied, giving his friend a stern look. "Do not goad me about this. I am not in the mood. Why do mothers make it their sole purpose to marry off their sons and daughters?"

Miles's lips curved. "Because they wish to have grandchildren." The man tensed upon seeing someone. "I too have been avoiding my mother's latest attempt at a match for me."

Following his friend's line of sight, two women walked through the room arm-in-arm, behind them the Duke of Spencer, Miles's father.

The women, one Lady Johnstone, the other a feminine version of Miles, although with softer features and was quite fetching had to be his sister, Penelope.

"Is this your sister's first Season?" Henry asked.

To his amusement, Miles's eyes narrowed. "I am afraid so. Already the vultures swarm."

"She is lovely," Henry said. "Why are you surprised."

"Because she is much too young and has informed my parents that she will not accept any suitors for at least another pair of seasons."

Unable to keep from it, Henry laughed. "Good for her."

"Indeed," Miles replied, not taking his eyes away from his sister, who was approached by a young man.

"I wish to dance." Felicity neared. "Have you seen Evan?"

"In the study with your father," Miles replied. "In a game of cards. May I have the pleasure?"

The pair walked off and soon Miles led Felicity around the room, the music enveloping them as Henry watched. To his consternation, his mother caught his eye and looked to Una.

Duty called and he crossed the salon and guided the delighted Una to the dancefloor.

"I wondered how long before you claimed your spots on my dance card," Una stated.

He'd not signed her card but had a good idea who had done it for him. With Una in his arms, they danced the waltz and, admittedly, he enjoyed it. Although he did not find himself attracted to Una, he did like to dance.

Whatever would it be like to dance with Hannah? He considered that once her mourning ended, he would be sure to invite her to a social event.

"Ouch!" Una yelped when he stomped on her foot. "We are not keeping up with the others," she added.

"Sorry." They fell into step and, at once, Una's hand inched around his shoulder so that they were closer than socially appropriate. The woman was relentless.

When the song ended, he guided Una toward where his mother had been, but she was no longer there. He searched the ballroom for where to deposit the woman. Una hung on his arm and smiled up at him. "I am parched. Would you be a dear and take us to find refreshment?"

"Where is your mother?"

"She did not come. I came with a chaperone. She is sitting either in the garden or in the solarium. Should we look?"

Henry nodded. "Of course."

Whoever the woman was, she was not in the solarium. After a turnabout the room, Henry made for the doorway. There had been plenty of couples caught in such places and forced into marriage and he did not intend to be one of them.

Admittedly, the fresh air of the garden was welcome. However, after looking to the area where benches had been set up for companions, Una announced that her chaperone was not there.

"Perhaps she went for a walk. The ninny can be quite thoughtless."

They walked a short distance away when Una stumbled forward. Henry caught her, and she met his gaze. "Thank you."

Before he could react, she kissed him full on the mouth, her arms entangled around his neck.

Henry kept his arms to his sides, but then had to take her by the shoulders to move her away.

"Oh dear," someone said, and he turned to find a pair of older women walking past.

"You should not have done that," Henry told Una, who gave him a dreamy look. "They will go inside and tell people about it."

It did not take long to figure out that it had been Una's plan all along, as when they made their way back toward the ballroom, an older woman appeared. "There you are Miss Una. I have been looking for you."

"I am in good company, as you can see, Millie. Do not fret." Una pulled him toward the ballroom.

Henry could barely keep from saying something untoward. Instead, he gritted his teeth and searched for his mother. Upon spotting her, they neared, and it was obvious she'd already heard about the kiss.

"We must speak directly upon arriving at home." His mother's gaze met his then Una's. "Are you well, dear girl?"

Una nodded, her cheeks pinkening. "I am unharmed, as you can see. It was but an innocent interval."

After making a feeble excuse, Henry hurried away to where

his friends stood. By their expressions, they'd also heard.

"Oh what now?" he asked upon nearing. "It was nothing more than something planned by her and my mother. I have no doubt."

"Her dowry will be enough that you will have the capital necessary for your portion of the sponsorship," Miles said dryly.

Henry fought the urge to punch him in the face. Especially when Evan's lips curved into a knowing look.

Evan grimaced. "You, my friend, may be caught in a web that will not be easy to escape."

"YOU ARE AVOIDING going home?" Miles said, giving Henry a curious look. "It is not often you suggest coming to my home."

They were in a townhouse that Miles currently lived in. Despite his parents' huge estate, the bachelor preferred to keep a more private home in the city. Miles would spend days at his family home, however it was more often that he resided in the city.

"The last place I wish to be is at my family home today. As you know, now that Evan is married, we cannot go there after social events. He and Felicity go directly to bed after and I don't wish to upset the household." Henry plopped down on a sofa and crossed his arms.

"You must get a piano and perhaps more liquor."

Miles poured them each a glass of brandy. "I will ensure to bring my home up to your standards."

"The kiss," Miles said. "Your mother and the young woman will seize the fact you were seen and insist on a marriage proposal."

Henry straightened. "Have you ever spent time with Una Stewart?"

"I have not had the pleasure."

"She is clingy, self-centered, and immature. I can only abide to be in her presence for short periods. And the family…they are the type who will do anything to be on the pages of all the gossips rags."

Crossing his legs at the ankles, Miles leaned back. "Sounds pretty much like every other family in our social class. If not for gossip and scandals, life would have little meaning."

Despite his sour mood, Henry chuckled. "You are correct, friend."

They remained quiet for a few moments. Miles finally stood. "You know where the spare bedroom is. Stay as many days as you please. I must retire. Tomorrow the search for my portion of the sponsorship begins anew. I met an interesting woman tonight. I have a good feeling."

"Good on you," Henry said, standing. "Thank you for the hospitality."

It was late the next morning by the time Henry left Miles's home. The cook had outdone herself and who was he to turn down the delicious full breakfast offerings?

Instead of heading to his home, where he was sure his mother awaited with some sort of ultimatum, he went to Hannah's.

Despite knowing it wasn't true, Henry convinced himself that the only reason for his visit was to be sure there were no new occurrences.

Marta was at the door, and after giving him a soft look, she opened it wider for him to pass.

"Mister Campbell. Miss Hannah is somewhere amongst the furniture." The woman walked away, weaving past chairs, tables, and other miscellaneous items.

"I must say. It does look much better," Hannah said from somewhere past the furniture. He made his way into the dining room that had been turned into some sort of shop. Silas polished a table as Hannah looked on holding a rag.

Her face brightened upon seeing him. "Good morning, Henry. As you can see, we are preparing the furniture for when the man you spoke about can come by."

It seemed Hannah had chosen to pretend the kiss between them had not happened. He steadied himself to ensure a neutral expression.

Walking into the space, he noted furniture had been separated and lined on opposite walls.

"You have certainly been busy the last couple of days," Henry said, astonished that she'd decided to take on the task amidst the current circumstances. Then again, it was probably a good way to keep her mind occupied.

She neared and accepted his kiss to her cheek. "When do you think the man can come?"

"I will seek him out today," he assured her, wishing Silas was not there so that he could hug her.

"Is something wrong?" Hannah asked, studying him. "You seem a bit preoccupied."

"I…um," he cleared his throat. "I am fine." Was it possible that he was in love? It couldn't be. Especially not now when he had so much to do.

Hannah tugged a chair closer to where Silas was. "What do you think? Keep or sell?"

The young man poked a finger into a hole in the upholstery. "Depends."

"Pooh! I did not notice that," Hannah said, inspecting the chair closer. "Sell."

After announcing it was enough for the moment and instructing Silas to finish polishing the table and another, she walked with him out of the room.

"What brings you?" She looked up to him, her eyes filled with curiosity. "Any news?"

"I will not know until after speaking with Evan. I spent the night at Miles' home and am just now out and about." They went into the parlor where a tray of tea awaited. Hannah lowered to sit and poured for them.

Her gaze moved to the French doors. "I had a fright last

night."

Immediately, he sat forward. "What happened?"

"Marta and Silas had gone so that she could visit her sister. The housekeeper was here. I was busy for hours searching for things in my father's study when I heard footsteps. I called out, but there was no answer. I practically fainted when I walked into the study and a man stood in the doorway. It was a constable who'd thought to have seen someone leaving the house and found the door open."

"Do you think someone was here?"

Hannah shook her head. "In all probability, it was the housekeeper leaving. I will have words with her about it. Especially if she left the side doors open after cleaning them."

"You definitely must speak to her about safety issues." Henry had an uneasy feeling. "Did the constable think it was a man or woman leaving your house?"

"He was too far to see. By the time he hurried closer, the person had turned the corner and he did not pursue them, wanting to come and ensure nothing was amiss here." She met his gaze. "Do not give me that look. I will not move in with Felicity or the Murrays."

"Someone inside your house while you were here alone is quite serious," Henry insisted. "Something has to be done."

Hannah stood and looked down at him. "It could have been Eileen that he saw. I refuse to live in fear. For all we know, this person is working on a supposition that the box is still here. Something perhaps said to him by a man on his death bed."

"He must believe it enough to take drastic steps. Otherwise, why would whoever it is hire McBean?"

"It doesn't matter. If not for it being lost all these years, for all he knows the money is spent. Whoever he is, the man is a fool."

Unable to keep from it, Henry stood. It was proving impossible not to keep from wishing to protect her above all things. It mattered not to him what his parents or anyone thought. If anything happened to Hannah, he would not forgive himself.

"You will go stay elsewhere or I will move in here."

Her mouth fell open and then, to his consternation, she laughed. "Henry, do not be like this. Please go home. I am not your responsibility. You never said why you came by today?"

The question took him by surprise. Swallowing past the lump that formed, he cleared his throat. "Because I care deeply for you. How can you ask?"

She looked down, her gaze traveling then to the doors. "I need to ask that you stop coming here. There is no need for it. Not only am I not your responsibility, but also, I believe we are becoming overly attached for which the only outcome will be hurt feelings. You and I cannot continue such a close friendship."

Obviously, she was distraught and unable to form clear thoughts. Henry let out a harsh breath. "I will speak to you tomorrow when you are more settled."

She stopped him from walking out with a hand on his upper arm. "No. You will not speak to me unless we happen upon one another at Felicity's. Do not return here."

When he met her gaze, he saw that she actually meant it. There was pleading in her expression, the depth of her emotions visible by the trembling of her bottom lip and welling of tears.

"Why?" was all he could formulate.

"Because I must protect myself. People have surely noticed your regular visits. Although I am not of your social stature, the gossips notice you and are already beginning to murmur about your visits. Besides, any assignation with me and all that happens will harm any chance of you finding a proper wife."

"Of course."

It wasn't until he mounted that Henry realized he'd left without the usual hug or kiss to the temple.

"Mister Campbell." A constable approached, his gaze going to the front of Hannah's house and then to him. "How is Miss Kerr this morning?"

"Unsettled," he replied and then dismounted. "Were you who saw the person leaving her house yesterday?"

The young man shook his head. "No, I work during the day only. I was told it was a tall person."

"Could it have been a woman?"

The young man shrugged. "I suppose, but we think a man."

"Thank you." Henry mounted again and rode away, unsure if he was prepared to face his mother and yet another unpleasant situation.

"THE STEWARTS ARE demanding action on your part to repair the damage done by your actions last night," his mother said as a way of greeting. "This must be seen to immediately. You must propose."

Henry stood in the doorway looking into the parlor where his mother set a stack of correspondence next to her. "I will not marry a woman who purposefully attempts to entrap me. It was her who acted and kissed me."

"You are a strong virile man, how can you possibly be accosted by a slip of a girl? Honestly, Henry." His mother shook her head. "It is time for you to settle. We cannot hope for a better match."

"I will speak to the Stewarts if you wish me to. I will explain to them that I will not be proposing to their daughter and offer my apologies. That is all I will do."

"Henry." His mother stood and walked to him, her gaze direct. "What exactly are you waiting for?"

The question was unsettling. "I will marry whom I choose and not because of circumstances that were an obvious ploy. I am not fully sure you were not involved in this plan."

His mother rolled her eyes. "There is no malicious plan at play, just your active imagination. You will pay a visit to the young lady and set things right."

CHAPTER NINE

HANNAH WAS GIDDY with excitement when the man Henry had recommended finally left with a cart full of furniture. He would return for a few pieces she preferred he repair.

The amount he'd paid was decent. Thanks to Marta, who'd haggled with him and gotten almost double what he'd first offered.

"Here." Hannah handed Marta a handful of notes. "Thank you."

The woman's eyes widened at the amount, her mouth falling open. "For me?"

"You earned it," Hannah said. "Do not use it to leave me."

Marta laughed. "I could never do that to you, Miss Hannah. You have lost too much already." The woman folded the notes, then pulled one. "I will give this to Silas for his help."

"There is something else I wish to speak to you about." Hannah motioned for Marta to sit. "I have been thinking. We should hire a permanent maid. You do too much, and I can afford one more person now."

The money from the box had been deposited at the bank. She was financially secure now, not having to pinch pennies or worry about repairs for the house or other things that had plagued her since her mother's departure.

"I do not mind," Marta said, looking around the kitchen. The woman was fiercely territorial. "Would this person live here?"

Hannah shrugged. "Not necessarily. Perhaps someone who

comes every day to help and leaves in the evening. I will need you to accompany me more, therefore there must be someone here."

"Very well. I will help you find someone."

WITH SILAS IN tow, Hannah rode in a hired carriage to Felicity's house. The butler greeted her warmly as she stepped into the parlor.

"Missus Macleod is in the sitting room."

Hannah entered the room and could sense something was wrong. Felicity let out a sigh and motioned to an empty chair. "I am so glad you're here. I could use the company."

"Is something wrong?" Hannah studied her friend's face.

Felicity smiled. "No, nothing really. I was just worried about you today. With all the rumors flying."

"I told him not to come back. It is not right for a bachelor to come calling all the time." Hannah smiled at Felicity. "I was becoming too attached."

Her friend's wide eyes met hers. "When did you see him? How did you hear?"

"This morning," Hannah replied. "I have not heard anything as of yet. But I knew sooner than later, the gossips would speculate about his visiting so often and alone."

"This morning," Felicity repeated, not meeting her gaze. "Hannah, that he visits is not what I'm referring to."

"What are you talking about?"

Just then a maid walked in with a tray. On it were two glasses of lemonade and dainty biscuits.

"Thank you, Rosalie," Felicity said, dismissing the woman.

"Something is wrong," Hannah said, her heart racing. "What happened?"

It was a few beats before Felicity seemed to gather her

thoughts. "Last night at the ball. Henry and Una Stewart were caught in a rather compromising state."

Immediately, her stomach plunged and her chest constricted. Hannah gasped. "What?"

"From what I heard, it was a rather passionate kiss and embrace. The women who happened upon them said it was a bit before Henry and Una even noticed their presence."

"I see. It is not surprising. The Stewarts are close friends of the Campbells, are they not?" It was as if she was not in her body but outside, watching what occurred. An empty version of herself sitting near Felicity, speaking as if all was well.

"I suppose," Felicity replied, studying her closely. "I am sorry. I know you care a great deal for Henry."

Hannah nodded. "This was going to happen sooner or later. Which is why I was stern with him this morning. What upsets me is that he did not tell me. He should have informed me. Instead, he acted as if all was the same. If anything, the fact he came to visit after what occurred angers me. How could he?"

To her shock, tears began to fall, trailing down her face unabated. Once again, she was to lose someone. How much more could she take?

"Promise you will never leave me." Hannah reached for Felicity's hand. "Promise."

A tear trickled down Felicity's cheek. "I promise. I will never, ever leave you."

Wiping tears away, they both sniffed at the same time. Hannah forced a smile. "Has the detective found out anything?"

"Evan is meeting with him this very afternoon." Her friend studied her for a long moment. "Tell me about the redecorating? I have something for you."

Felicity stood, pulled a cord, and moments later George appeared. "Yes, Missus?"

"Be a dear and bring the bolts of fabric that were delivered," Felicity asked the man who hurried away.

Moments later, he appeared with Silas, who carried four bolts of different fabrics. It was obvious Felicity did what she could to distract her and, for the moment, Hannah allowed it.

"They are beautiful." Hannah examined each one. "What are you planning to do with them?"

Her friend gave her a mischievous look. "I saw them when I visited Evan at work the other day. I asked for four. With two, I will have draperies made for the upstairs and gift you two bolts for your house."

Hannah smiled, her mood lifting just a bit. "I will be using this one in the parlor." She touched one with a floral design in corals and greens. The other was a bit darker with a design of a fleur-de-lis. "Dining room."

They spent the rest of the afternoon having a leisurely meal while discussing Hannah's plans for redecoration and they decided Felicity would return with Hannah to her house and await Evan.

IT WAS NEARLY midnight before Hannah went to bed. She'd spent the evening annoyed that although the detective had found out information about Jules Brown, Evan refused to tell either her or Felicity anything. He was afraid they'd go off and try to find him themselves, which in actuality, was not much of a stretch.

Upon arriving home, Marta waited with two women who wished to apply for the maid position. In the end, she'd hired the younger one, mostly because she needed the job more.

The house was too quiet now, and Hannah wondered if it had always been so. When living there with her parents, it did not seem so. At least she never considered it to be eerily silent like it was in that moment.

Throwing the blankets off, she went to the window and peered out. There was nothing or no one on the street. Through the darkness she spotted a small figure trotting into the yard and sniffing around. A dog perhaps.

She threw on her robe and hurried down the stairs. In the kitchen, she grabbed a piece of leftover meat and hurried out the back door into the garden.

Upon spotting her, a small dog lifted its head and made a noise, something akin to a growl. Being it was either a tiny breed or a puppy, it wasn't at all intimidating.

"Here, sweet. Have this." Hannah broke off small pieces and tossed them close to the dog. Although wary, the dog gobbled up each piece then waited for another.

Bit by bit, she kept feeding it until it neared. Lowered to the ground in a pose of submission, the animal neared, its head low.

"You need a friend, do you not?" Hannah said, sliding her hand over the furry pup. It was a young dog, no more than a few months old. "How did you end up here all alone?"

Startling the animal, she scooped it up and brought it into the kitchen. Then after warming milk, she set a bowl of it on the floor.

The little dog lapped the milk, its tail wagging with happiness.

After finding an old blanket, she folded it, placed it in a corner of the room, and left. The dog would have a warm and safe place to sleep for the night.

Moments later as she once again peered out the window, the pup entered her bedroom and gazed up at her. Perhaps she imagined it, but there was gratitude in the dog's gaze that melted her heart.

"Fine, you can stay here tonight." She lifted the little creature to the settee on the end of her bed. After a few circles, the pup settled and fell into a content slumber.

Once again, she climbed into bed. The truth of the matter was that she was avoiding it because immediately, the fact of losing Henry became real. Although it was not unexpected that he would find himself attracted to someone and having to marry.

There had been no time to prepare. After asking him to not visit as often, she'd expected a few months at least to prepare herself for the inevitable.

But on the very day? That had been totally unexpected. Yes, she loved Felicity like a sister, but her friend had no idea how much the news of Henry's kiss with Una Steward would affect her. Or it could be she did and that was why she made sure to tell her immediately.

Giving into the pain, Hannah turned to her side and cried. Life was so very cruel. And yet, there she was still in the middle of it, doing her best to live each day, to survive past every circumstance.

Her mother's disclosure, strangers demanding things, someone in her house, and yet, she had refused to buckle. Her body shook when she gave into the sadness that enveloped. Henry would no longer be there for her and just the thought of it tore through her.

Just then, shifting beside her caught her attention. With a soft whimper, the little dog nestled against her back. Hannah swallowed a cry. It had to be her father who'd sent the small creature to comfort her in his stead.

"MISS HANNAH, YOU have a visitor. You've slept in." Marta opened the curtains, brightening the room. "Should I ask that they return later?"

"Who?" Hannah sat up and looked around. "Where is the dog?"

Marta gave her a stern look. "The animal is downstairs making herself right at home. She's been bathed and fed."

"Oh good." Hannah smiled, knowing Marta, like her, had a heart for animals. "Who is downstairs?"

"A detective. Sent by Mister Macleod."

Flinging back the blankets, Hannah slipped from the bed. "Serve him tea. I will be down momentarily. Do not let him leave."

Moments later, she hurried into the parlor to find an older bearded man drinking tea. The man stood. "Garrett Baxter, Miss."

"Good morning," Hannah said and sat down. "I am glad to see you."

"Unfortunately, I do not bring an uplifting report. I found the man, Jules Brown. He lives alone in a rather questionable section of town and seems to keep unsuitable company."

When Marta came to the doorway, Hannah motioned for her to join them. "What can you tell me about him?"

"What I informed Mister Macleod is that Mister Jules Brown has taken over Horace Brown's business. Which is the ownership of several gambling dens."

Marta gasped. "Most unholy of places."

"Indeed," Mister Baxter agreed. "From what I could find out, he is not in need of money and does not seem to be ailing."

"How old is he?" Hannah asked.

The detective thought about it. "Ah yes, I failed to describe him. Mister Brown is twenty-three, has brown hair and eyes. He is of medium build and about my height."

"I see," Hannah said, considering that Jules Brown was two years older than her. "I will need his address."

The man seemed uncomfortable at disclosing the information. "Mister Macleod asked that I tell you he plans to pay Jules Brown a visit."

"The address, sir," Hannah insisted. "This is my family. I have reason to believe Jules Brown is my half-brother."

"What are you going to do?" Marta asked once the detective left.

"I am going to pay Jules Brown a visit this very afternoon." Hannah turned to the door. "Now let me see my little dog. I shall have to name her."

In the kitchen while Hannah sat on the floor to play with the pup, Marta fretted in the background.

Hannah studied the brown-speckled pup. "I know. You will be called Betty."

The dog licked her hand, seeming to like the name.

"Miss Hannah, you should speak to Mister Macleod about this. Or perhaps Mister Henry."

"Mister Henry will not be visiting any longer. From what I hear, he has other issues to see about." Hannah looked to the woman and smiled. "I have to learn to fend for myself. I have no family to help."

"The man sounds dangerous."

Knocks sounded and both looked to the doorway. Marta hurried to answer the door while Hannah attempted to catch the pup. It slipped from her grasp, raced to the front door, and barked. The dog's high-pitched barks would not scare anyone away.

Marta turned to look at her and held out a note.

"Thank you," Hannah said, taking the note with her to the parlor. Upon sitting, she opened it. It was from Felicity asking that she not do anything impetuous. She further informed that both Evan and Lord Johnstone would be paying Jules Brown a visit.

There was no word as to when. Hannah surmised it would not be for a day or two. The men liked to preplan everything.

With a long sigh, she folded the note and turned to the view of the garden. She could not continue to wait. The sooner everything was resolved, the faster she could move on with her life.

Hannah went out of the parlor, down the corridor, and up the stairs. While perusing the clothes in the chifforobe, she considered that she wasn't exactly sure what one wore to visit a rather unpleasant side of town.

CHAPTER TEN

HENRY STALKED INTO the parlor, prepared to face his parents and whoever else was there. Although he knew Una was in all probability in cahoots with his mother, he had to make sure to tread carefully and not allow his temper to get the best of him.

There were more important things to do in an afternoon than to be told whom to marry by mothers who had nothing better to dedicate their time to.

Sitting in the room were both his mother and Lady Stewart, who he'd never particularly cared for. The woman was judgmental and constantly bringing gossip to his mother.

"Young man," the woman began. "I find it deplorable that you made your mother and I wait even a minute. This matter of what happened between you and my daughter must be seen to immediately. An engagement will be the only way to quiet the tongues."

He kept quiet. Otherwise he'd point out it was she who had the loosest of tongues, except for Lady Wilshire, who was beyond compare.

"What do you have to say, Henry?" his mother asked with an impatient motion for him to sit. "Don't just stand there, son."

Still standing, he eyed the scones on the tray. The cook made the most delicious scones, and he would go in search of one once the current matter was settled.

First he met his mother's gaze and then Lady Stewart's. "I am not going to be trapped into marriage. It was Una who kissed me, not the other way around. She waited until someone was nearing. I am not totally convinced you did not have something to do with it, Mother."

The women exchanged astounded looks.

"Henry, you are a well-built man, how could you expect us to believe my daughter accosted you against your will." Lady Stewart shook her head.

He blew out a calming breath. "She kissed me. I did not say accosted. Nevertheless, I will not marry Una. My heart belongs to someone else."

At the announcement, his mother's eyes rounded. "What? Who?"

"That is a discussion I prefer to speak about at a later time. If you ladies will excuse me, Father expects me to meet with him about a contract and I must go."

Lady Stewart stood. "You must make this right. How can you be so cavalier about my daughter's reputation?"

"It is not I who acted without considering the consequences, Lady Stewart. I hold you and your family in high esteem and would not deliberately set out to hurt any of you. However, that does not mean that I will bind myself to a woman I do not love, for life. You must explain this to Una."

Before either could speak, he walked directly out the front door where his horse awaited. Upon mounting, he rode from the property refusing to look back. Hopefully his mother and Lady Stewart would give up on the idea.

Once he met with his father and business colleague, he had to speak to Hannah. It had been two days since he'd seen her. After a night of wondering what to do and avoid a marriage that would no doubt make him miserable, he had to come up with a way to convince Hannah to marry him.

The building where he was to meet his father was at the end of the main street quite close to the Grant Hotel he frequented. Henry dismounted and handed the reins to a waiting steward.

"Where is my father?" he asked upon entering and was ushered into a large study.

His father eyed him silently, obviously noting he was late to arrive.

"There is no one else here," Henry pointed out. "Whoever we are to meet are later than me."

"What happened?"

"Mother and Lady Stewart demand that I marry Una to make up for being seen with her in the garden. It is utterly ridiculous."

His father frowned. "You should make amends, son. You cannot go about making inappropriate advances without expecting repercussions."

"Father, I did not kiss the woman. She planned the entire thing. Not only will I not marry her because obviously she is devious, but also because I plan to ask Miss Kerr to accept my courtship."

At the sound of footsteps, his father refrained from replying.

THROUGHOUT THE BUSINESS discussion, Henry noted that his father deferred to him more than once. The information he relayed was not difficult, but at the same time, it was obvious his father had not read over the details.

Finally, they came to an agreement and documents were signed and witnessed.

"A word," his father said as the men they'd met with walked out. "Sit down."

Henry waited, prepared to defend his decisions both about the business transaction and the marriage situation. The fact his parents were in an arranged marriage meant they did not understand his need to make the decision based on more than social compatibility.

"Did the detective find out anything?"

"Yes, I believe the man, Jules Brown, owns gambling dens

and is financially secure. He lives on the outskirts of town near one of the dens. Interesting that he wishes to find the box when it is evident he does not need the money."

"Greed perhaps." His father templed his fingers, his gaze traveling about the room while considering the information. "We should pay this Mister Brown a visit."

Henry sat straighter. "What would we possibly say to the man? It could be dangerous to try to warn him off."

The familiar gleam of curiosity shined in his father's eyes. "We could go under the pretense of a business dealing and get a sense of what the man is about. I have considered purchasing a building to be used as a clinic for young mothers."

"Young mothers?"

"Never mind that. What do you think? Let us get the carriage and go."

"What did you think about the percentage I negotiated?" Henry asked, since his father did not broach the subject.

"Yes, well, unfortunately I was unable to review things as your mother had me out so late at the dinner party last night. It is refreshing that I can rely on you now. I am impressed, son. Thoroughly impressed."

ALTHOUGH HE OFTEN rode with his father to different locations to conduct business or attend social functions, Henry could not help but sense the unsaid topic between them as the carriage rambled over the uneven cobblestone street. From what he gathered, the ride would not be a long one, just enough time to speak about what had occurred before he'd left the family home that morning.

"Father, Lady Stewart was at the house. Both she and mother insist that I am responsible for what occurred in the garden between Una Stewart and myself."

Lord Campbell nodded. "As you are well aware, son, we have

a close relationship with the Stewarts. Your mother was most put out that you have not taken initiative in this. What exactly happened?"

Once again, he repeated the situation in the garden, emphasizing that he'd not only not initiated the kiss, but had not participated by any way in the embrace. His father's chuckle was annoying, but Henry let it pass. "I refuse to marry this woman. She is manipulative. I am not attracted to her in the least."

"You know it matters little what actually happened compared to what is perceived. As you should already be aware, son, it is always best to avoid any situation that could bring these kinds of repercussions."

His father's words did not help in the least.

Hopefully another scandal would occur that would take the attention away from anyone who considered this to be high on the list of the gossipmongers.

The carriage slowed and his father's lips curved. "This will be quite interesting."

"Ensure to not draw unnecessary attention. The man cannot suspect that we are here for anything other than the issue of purchasing the building," Henry said.

"I am a sleuth," his father replied. "Subterfuge is my specialty."

Henry coughed to cover laughter. "Yes, of course."

His father was neither of those things. If anything, Henry was prepared for the worst.

As he'd expected a menacing sort at the door, Henry was surprised when a woman dressed in a serviceable navy gown greeted them and invited them to a sitting area. The small salon was decorated in a style that one would not expect in that part of town.

There were several paintings on the walls, thick draperies, and ornate tables. The chairs were upholstered in what he recognized to be expensive fabrics.

"Mister Lewiston H. Campbell here to speak to Mister

Brown," his father said in way of greeting. He motioned to Henry. "My son, Henry Campbell."

"I will see if Mister Brown is available," she replied in a prim tone and quickly walked away.

"I expected thugs," his father said, looking to where the woman disappeared past a doorway.

"Shh." Henry gave him a sharp look, which his father ignored.

There were knocks on the front door. The sharp raps seemed to echo in the large space.

Just as Henry wondered if anyone was to answer the door, a man appeared. This one did fit the part of whom they'd expected to greet them. With a broken nose and huge meaty hands, the man looked like a street boxer. He gave them a cursory glance before continuing to the door.

"What?" he said to whoever it was.

It sounded as if the visitor was a woman. The man turned to look past them in the direction the woman had gone. "You'll have to wait."

Whoever it was spoke again and the man huffed. "Very well, wait inside." He motioned to where Henry and his father sat.

A moment later, Hannah and her housekeeper Marta walked in. Both of their eyes rounded at seeing them. Luckily, they were facing away from the man who'd let them in.

"You have to wait for Rebecca to return. Although I doubt Mr. Jones will see you today." The man's eyes narrowed in Henry's direction, and he walked to a desk that he assumed was the woman's and sat on the edge.

"What are you doing here?" Hannah whispered.

"Young lady," his father began, and Henry held his breath. "We have business with Mister Brown. However, we will strive to be brief."

Hannah seemed struck speechless.

Glancing toward the man, Henry was about to speak when the woman, Rebecca, reappeared. She stopped upon seeing

Hannah and Marta.

"She says to have an important matter to discuss with Mister Brown," the man said to Rebecca, who slid a look to Hannah.

Henry took advantage and pretended to brush his pants leg. "You must not meet with him alone," he muttered under his breath.

"You have no reason to be involved in this any longer," she snapped back.

Rebecca's head turned toward them. "Mister Campbell, Mister Brown is occupied, but he asks that you wait a moment," she said to his father.

Knocks interrupted whatever she was about to say next. "I'll see to it," the man said, but she shook her head. "Go and see if Mister Brown is available yet." She hurried to the door in what seemed to be her efficient way of walking.

Whoever was at the door seemed to catch Rebecca by surprise. She turned to look at the four of them. "Please come in, Lord Johnstone."

Miles walked in and hesitated at seeing the group gathered. His right brow lifting, he turned to Evan who appeared next.

It was becoming rather crowded in the sitting room. The man and woman that worked for Jules exchanged confused looks and then turned to them.

"It was hard for Henry not to look at his companions, but instead, he kept his gaze on the duo. There was no doubt in his mind that Jules Brown was dangerous, and by the size of the man standing before them, it could be a formidable threat if he became suspicious."

Footsteps sounded and all eight people turned to watch as a man appeared. The man, who Henry presumed to be Jules Brown, had the assured gait of a man aware he was untouchable. His hair was dark and so were his eyes.

Behind him, two men who looked like prize fighters flanked him.

Jules ignored everyone except for Hannah. "You came."

To his consternation, Hannah walked up to Jules and pressed a finger to the center of his chest. "Of course I came. You have been sending undesirables to approach my housekeeper and had us followed."

When Henry took a step forward, prepared to defend Hannah, his father held him back.

"We should speak in private." For the first time, Jules seemed to notice everyone else. "Leave." He motioned to the men. "See everyone else except for the housekeeper out."

"I would prefer if they stayed," Hannah said. "They are my friends, who came here without my knowledge to try and keep me safe."

Jules's jaw flexed. "I am the one who gives orders here."

"And I am your sister and will not be bossed about."

At the words, Jules's eyes went wide. "What?"

"Mother admitted to me that when she married my father, she was with child. She gave you up because she feared your father and hoped to keep it a secret."

It was obvious when he went silent that Jules was processing the information. Hannah met his gaze and let out a sigh, quickly averting her eyes to the others present.

"There is nothing else to say. Leave," Jules said, his hands curling into fists.

Not for the first time, Hannah showed an extreme quiet valor. She looked up to the threatening man with a soft expression. "You killed my father or had him killed and he was innocent. Neither he nor Mother had any idea where the box was hidden. The housekeeper who hid it took the secret to her grave. I found it and brought it."

Marta held out a bundle and unwrapped it to show the box.

"What was in it?" Jules asked, motioning for one of his men to take the box. "Did you find anything?"

Hannah nodded. "Yes, money. It is in the bank. If you promise to leave all of us alone, I will have it brought to you."

"I have no need for the money," Jules spat out. "I want something she took from my father."

The box was placed on a surface and opened to show that indeed it was empty. Jules approached it and closed the lid. He traced the surface as if following a pattern and then pressed his finger to one spot.

A panel fell open and inside was a key.

He took it and held it up, then seeming to remember he had an audience, returned his attention to Hannah.

"You will not be bothered. You have my word."

Hannah met Jules's gaze for a long moment. "I cannot forgive you."

Not sure what she'd do next, Henry went to her side. "Come, let's go."

They all walked out in silence. Two men followed them to the door.

"If you ever need anything, Hannah," Jules said.

Hannah did not reply; instead, she huffed.

"Miss Hannah," Marta sniffed, taking one of her hands. "You were so brave."

"I daresay, we still do not know what the key is for," his father muttered. "In all possibility, larger coffers."

Miles and Evan neared. "We will take you home," Evan said to Hannah. "Our carriage is here."

"I was about to offer," Henry countered. "Hannah?"

"I will go with Evan. You have matters to see to from what I hear." Not looking to him, she walked toward the waiting carriage. It was evident the encounter with Jules had affected her and, once alone, she would succumb to emotions. She'd been terrified and had been brave only because she had no one but herself to protect her household.

"If you do not mind, I will go with you," Miles said to Henry, his eyes trailing Hannah and the others. "Brave woman."

CHAPTER ELEVEN

HANNAH WANTED TO be left alone to grieve, to sleep, and to not speak to anyone. However, she was at Felicity's once again. Everyone insisted on taking care of her. She'd been given a sweetened tea for her nerves and then forced to eat. But that wasn't enough for her friend, who was eager to ensure her wellbeing.

She'd been brought to a bedroom with a hot bath awaiting, perfumed oils in the water that were supposed to be soothing. Once that was done, she'd dressed in a warm gown and wrapped in a plush robe and now sat in a chair in front of a fireplace with another cup of tea at her elbow.

Through it all she'd been unable to utter a single word. Her mind whirled, every instance of the visit to Jules Brown repeating.

He was her brother, and he was a murderer. Whether he'd killed her father with his own hands or paid someone to do it did not matter.

There had been a sort of familiarity in him that had shocked her. They favored in more ways than not. But there was a hardness in Jules that spoke of a life so very different from hers. If she were to guess, he'd grown up on the streets having to fight for everything until he found his father.

How that had occurred did not matter to her. What did was the fact that he'd never pay for his part in her father's murder. Men like Jules Brown bought judges and other authorities. He was no doubt untouchable.

All because of a key. A stupid key.

Her father had died, and she'd been abandoned for a key.

"Hannah?"

Felicity walked into the room with a tray. "I brought you some soup. Please eat it. Then I promise to leave you alone to rest."

"You have fed me more today than the entirety of what I've eaten in a week."

Her friend laughed softly. "You should eat more then."

As her friend kept her company, she ate a bit of the soup. Admittedly, it was delicious and warmed her.

"I am not sure what to do," Hannah said. "How do I continue on knowing that my father's killer will continue to enjoy his life, not paying for what he did?"

"I doubt that anyone who kills another person ever truly enjoys their life. I refuse to believe it," Felicity explained.

Hannah sighed. "There are people with hearts of stone that do not feel anything."

Having looked into Jules's eyes, Hannah wasn't sure she could say he was without emotion. There had been a flicker of something when she'd spoken of her father dying in vain. Had he felt anything?

"Do you think you will ever hear from him?" Felicity asked.

She shrugged. "I doubt it. I prefer not to. He is a criminal. A man whom I never wish to see or know about ever." Hannah let out a long breath and closed her eyes. "I hope to be able to sleep without thinking of him. I want to forget he exists."

"Of course," Felicity said, standing.

Once in bed, her thoughts took a drastic turn. Instead of thinking of Jules, she considered that Henry and his father had been there at Jules's offices. It had been a shock to walk in and see them. Marta had gasped audibly.

Why had he been there? Was it because of his need to be her champion, still clutching to the responsibility he'd felt since finding her father?

After what occurred, knowing that finally he would belong to someone else, her already frayed nerves had threatened to unravel fully at seeing him.

He'd come to stand beside her, a show that she was not alone but had plenty of support. Not only him, but Evan and Lord Johnstone had been there silently at her back. Jules must have understood that she had strong allies. Just thinking of it brought tears of gratitude. She was indeed fortunate for Felicity and the support she'd amassed on her behalf.

Although, if Hannah were to be honest, Henry had been her strongest support from the first.

Now she had to become accustomed to his absence. First thing in the morning, she'd speak to Evan and ask that he meet with Henry and explain that she wishes him well but asks that he not ever visit or approach her again.

With a shaky breath, she looked up at the ceiling. In a way, it felt good to know she'd protected herself and her household. Despite everything, she believed Jules. He got what he was after and would not bother her again.

Funny that she'd always wished for siblings. As the saying went, "Be careful what you wish for" was certainly true in her case.

MORNING CAME AND, to Hannah's surprise, she felt refreshed. Although she was reluctant to have to face other people, she dressed and combed her hair. When looking in the mirror, she noted that although a bit pale, she did look well-rested. It could be that without the threat, she was able to sleep better.

"Good morning," Felicity greeted her in the corridor. "I was just about to come and fetch you for breakfast. Cook has outdone herself, it smells lovely."

They went to the dining room where Evan already sat. He stood and held out a chair for his wife and then for Hannah.

"Were you able to sleep well?" he asked her and Hannah nodded.

"After the teas, food, and bath, I slept like a babe."

"I am glad to hear it," he replied with a smile.

"We must move forward. Perhaps plan a lady's tea here," Felicity said. "I do not wish to pressure you, but the sooner we move forward, the better for you."

The underlying reason was of course that Henry was to marry soon, and Felicity tried to distract her from it.

In actuality, the thought of it broke her heart. Each time she remembered what had occurred between Henry and another woman, it was as if her entire body split into pieces.

"Yes. I agree, it is best to move forward and begin my new life. It seems I will be living alone for the time being."

Felicity nodded. "With Marta as a companion, all should be well. What about perhaps hiring a butler?"

"No," Hannah replied. "I do not feel comfortable with men under my employ. Silas is enough. I have hired a maid."

It was afternoon by the time she and Marta returned home. She was excited at the prospect of continuing with redecorating the house. It had been a relief that Jules had not wanted the money, because without it, things would have been harder for her.

Now as she walked into the disorganized house, all she saw were possibilities.

"I will change into something more serviceable. In the meantime, put the items that will be fixed near the front door," she said to Silas.

By the time the men arrived, and furniture was loaded and taken away; the sitting room and dining room were bare except for the main table.

"My goodness," Marta said. "Where will you eat until the chairs are returned?"

"In the parlor. Let us set up a table with two chairs for meals." They went to the parlor and moved a round table to one side of the room near the French doors. Then they brought a matching set of chairs from her father's office and put them on either side.

Hannah covered the table with a large square embroidered cloth and in the center placed a vase. "I will cut some flowers. Can you fetch tea? I am famished."

"It looks lovely," Marta said and hurried away.

With little Betty at her heels, seeming to find interesting smells in every corner of the garden, Hannah walked about and snipped flowers for the vase. Flowers she and her mother had tended over the years bloomed brightly despite the dire need for tending. With a sigh, Hannah realized she looked forward to the task of gardening. The more to keep her occupied the better.

"You look beautiful today." Henry's voice fell over her and she fought not to turn and face him. Her chest constricted and Hannah blinked, attempting to keep from crying.

"Why are you here? Did you not get my message? Felicity said it would be delivered today."

He walked closer. Despite her not looking at him, she caught sight of his booted foot. "I did, which is why I am here."

"Please, Henry." Hannah finally turned to him. It took her breath to see him. He was the only man she'd ever love, and now alone with him, all she could think was how much she missed him and needed his touch.

"I am not going to marry her. I've made it clear to her family. I cannot, will not marry someone I do not care for or am not attracted to."

The basket forgotten, Hannah hurried to the side of the house where passersby would not see her. Her chest heaved with deep gulps of air.

"What happened, are you unwell?" Henry neared and held her by the upper arms. "Hannah?"

"I have to move on. Don't you see? You cannot continue to

come. It makes it harder."

From behind him, she caught sight of Marta, who looked on with understanding and then walked away. She'd give them privacy, for which Hannah was thankful.

"I miss you when I do not see you. I think about you daily. It is how I have concluded that I am in love with you, Hannah Kerr." Henry lifted her face and searched her eyes. "I cannot imagine not seeing you every single day."

"We both know it can never be between us."

Henry pressed his lips to hers. "You feel as strongly. I know you do." He whispered against her mouth, his breath fanning over hers.

What did it matter what she felt? The truth of the matter was they could never be. Even if he decided not to marry the woman in question. His family ties meant he had to be careful who he did marry.

"I cannot allow this," Hannah replied, although relenting and melting against him as the familiar sense of Henry filled her. There would never be another man who would make her feel like him. Someone who would send her reeling, overwhelming every bit of her being.

Knowing it would in all probability be the last time she'd ever see him, Hannah reached for his face, cupping his jaw with her palm. "Why does it have to be so difficult to let you go? But I must. I absolutely must, or I will go mad if you continue to come here."

His mouth crashed against hers and her hand slipped from his jaw to around his neck. The kiss became passionate. The feel of his body against her engulfing hers with a heat like none she'd ever felt before.

Hannah raked her fingers through Henry's hair, reveling in the softness. When his tongue pressed against the seam of her lips, she parted eagerly. Once in her mouth, he traced the roof of her mouth and she shivered from the sensations that traveled down her spine.

When the pads of his fingers on the side of her throat traced a circular pattern, the caress was much too exquisite to push his hand away. Instead, she leaned her head to the left, relinquishing more.

Henry broke the kiss but kept his lips on hers, then trailed ever so slowly to her jawline, pressing softly against the now overly sensitive skin.

She clung to him with desperation, not wanting him to ever stop, but instead for time to stand still and allow this moment to last forever.

It was as if his lips were fevered, the heat emanating as he continued the combination of caresses and kisses. To her jaw, then up to just below the ear where he lingered, his tongue darting out to taste.

Hannah gasped when his mouth pressed against the side of her neck, the ground shifting under her feet. "Oh." It was the only word that escaped because any others would break the spell.

By the time his lips trailed to her shoulder, Hannah was trembling, barely able to keep tears at bay. At the same time, heat filled her, pooling in the most private part of her. She could not ask that he stop. Instead, she fought not to beg he continue. Something had to quench the fire inside.

"Trust me," Henry said and lowered before her. "Shh."

"What are you doing?" Hannah fought to keep from collapsing onto the ground and begging that he do something to stop the blaze that burned so hot.

He looked up at her and rose again, only he trailed his hand up her leg, lifting the skirt of her dress.

"Oh," she gasped. Once again, he took her mouth. Was it possible he knew? Understood what was happening to her body, the absolute need that raged. The fire that burned so hot it threatened to engulf her completely.

"I will take care of you. I promise." His darkened eyes met hers for a moment, his hand resting on her upper leg. "Close your eyes."

Hannah gripped his shoulders and obeyed. Once again, his mouth covered hers, and she enjoyed the kiss, but couldn't keep from concentrating on the fact that his hand touched her leg.

When Henry deepened the kiss, she gave in, but only for a moment because in the next instant, his fingers slipped between the folds of her sex.

"Ah!"

Thankfully, his mouth covered hers because what he did next sent her reeling.

With nimble moves, he circled the nub at the center of her sex, his mouth still covering hers, sending tendrils of what she could only describe as liquid fire down her legs. Each movement of his fingers was like adding flames to the already blazing heat and she could only cling to him, on the verge of begging that he never stop.

Unable to keep from it, she pushed into this hand, too lost to consider her actions.

"Please," she managed to whisper against his lips.

"Shh," Henry said and then did the simplest of things. With rapid movements, he glided the tip of his finger over a single spot over and over.

It was as if a dam burst and Hannah lost all control. Her body splintered into fragments time and time again until she dissolved into a heap of nothing but flesh.

Unless held up by him, she was sure to have fallen to the ground. Hannah pressed her face into his shoulder as she fought to regain control.

"What have you done?" she managed to say. "Have you spoiled me?"

"No." Henry's tone was strong. "Never. It was just what can be brought on by caresses."

Taking a fortifying breath, Hannah pushed back, praying her shaky knees held her upright. "It should not have happened."

"But it did. We will marry." Henry stated and pressed a kiss to her parted lips. "Soon because I cannot be patient and must be with you fully."

She understood of course what he meant. However, she was not about to allow anything as foolish to happen again.

The aftermath of their intimate moment made her breathless and yet, she fought to keep her voice stable. "We will not. You know very well what it would mean for your family. Your parents will never allow it." She held up a hand when he started to speak. "No matter what you say to me in this moment, upon reflection, you know I am right. I must forget you. You must forget about me."

"Do you not love me?" Henry took her by the shoulders and stared into her eyes. "I love you, Hannah."

The words were like a sweet nectar sliding down one's throat ever so slowly. "I do love you, Henry. I admit it. Have loved you for longer than I cared to admit, even to myself. However, how we feel does not change the reality of our circumstance. I would bring scandal. None of it my fault, but at the same time, a very strong reason for not marrying me."

"I will not stop fighting until you are my wife." He gave her a pointed look. "Tell me you will marry me once all is cleared up."

A tear slipped down her cheek. The man she loved so dearly stood before her, meaning every word that he said. However, both knew it could never be. She would only bring shame and troubles into his family.

"Promise not to return," Hannah said, brushing the tear away. "Please."

Henry looked away for a moment. "How can I convince you to wait for me?"

"I will not allow you to do this to your family. For you to disappoint your parents in such a manner that you marry a woman who brings with her a questionable murder, a brother who is a criminal, and a mother who abandoned her to live alone as a single woman."

"This conversation is not over." He pressed a kiss to her lips. "Wait for me."

In a stupor, Hannah walked to where the basket lay on the ground and lowered to pick up the blooms. Then she collapsed onto the ground, sitting still while holding a flower.

Something had to be done. Perhaps she could leave for the rest of the Season. Go visit her aunt and find out if all was well. There still had not been a response to her letter.

If she remained away for a time, then Henry would hopefully move on. Not being there would be helpful as well. She would not hear any news about him or chance running into him.

"Marta," Hannah called out as she entered the house. "Help me pack."

***

"I CANNOT BELIEVE you were thinking of leaving," Felicity said, lifting a cup of tea to her lips. "Honestly, Hannah. You must remain here; there is so much to see to. Besides, I need you."

Hannah almost laughed. "You do not need me. You have Evan, Grant, and your mother."

"Yes, well, Grant is gone, as you know, in hopes of fleecing some rich old woman of money." Felicity shook her head. "If I am to be honest, whoever doesn't see through his ruse deserves it. Why would a young man wish to be with someone old enough to be their grandmother? It makes me shudder."

"I don't understand this quest of theirs for funding. None of them, especially Lord Johnstone, have need of it."

"It is a bet. Once men set about this sort of thing, there is no talking them out of it. More of a competition to see who manages to get the funds."

It was a moment before Hannah spoke. "And Henry, where is he getting the money?"

Felicity's right shoulder lifted and lowered. "Probably from his father. I do believe they have been working quite close together." Her friend's eyes narrowed. "You have yet to explain your sudden urge to flee."

"How is it between a man and a woman…when making love?" Hannah asked, avoiding the topic.

Although she was sure her friend would not divulge the intimate details, it was easy to understand that her friend enjoyed bedsport. In a matter of seconds, Felicity's face softened and there was a slight pinking to her cheeks. "When with the right man, I surmise, it will be most enjoyable. It is as if the entire world disappears until there is only him." Felicity sighed.

"That did not answer my question," Hannah said, sitting up straighter. "I mean physically. What goes where?"

"Oh." Felicity frowned. "I am not sure I should tell you such detail."

"We promised whoever married first would tell the other. Remember?" Hannah replied. "I am interested because, well…I may never marry and would like to know."

Felicity stood and went to the doorway. She pulled the sliding doors closed and then returned to sit. "What happens is, well at first you kiss. Then it becomes rather…well you know… passionate."

When her friend paused, Hannah didn't dare say anything, fearing Felicity would lose her nerve.

"His sex member becomes hardened, and he enters you. At first, it's a bit uncomfortable. In truth, it hurt. As you continue moving, then it becomes better." Felicity stopped. "That's it."

"It sounds awful." Hannah bit her bottom lip. "I do not think I would like it at all." She considered that whatever Henry did was much more enjoyable. It did not cause any pain whatsoever.

"It is not awful," Felicity said. "There is movement. You join and move and eventually you fly."

"Fly?"

"Float."

"How do you do that?" Hannah asked, picturing a couple levitating over the bed.

"Not physically," Felicity replied with a giggle. "Emotionally, mentally. Your body bursts into flames; it is most wonderful."

At the mention of flames, Hannah understood. "Oh, I see. Interesting."

"One day you will find out and we will laugh about this conversation."

Hannah studied Felicity, who she loved more than life itself. "You are not very good at describing things."

"You have a dreamy look about you. Did something happen? Is Henry the reason for this sudden wish to leave Glasgow?"

Hannah shook her head. "In part, yes. I do not wish to see him. It pains me to know he will marry another. Then there is the fact that my aunt has not responded. She could be very ill or worse. I want to find out."

CHAPTER TWELVE

HENRY WAS PREPARED to set things straight. There were two very important matters that had to be dealt with, and upon speaking to his father, hopefully both would be solved.

His footsteps echoed on the pristine floor that led to his father's study. He'd just walked out a business acquaintance with whom his father just concluded working with. The venture had made both men quite a handsome return.

This was the opportune moment to approach his father, as the patriarch would be in a jovial mood.

"Henry," his father said upon him entering. "Make sure to meet with the bankers in the morning to deposit the funds."

"I will." Henry poured brandy into two glasses and handed one to his father. "To profit and good business."

They held the glasses up and then drank.

"I must revisit something with you," Henry said, meeting his father's gaze. "The matter of a loan in order for me to invest in a ship that departs in a pair of months. I have been able to come up with a portion, but it is doubtful without your help I will have the money in time."

"Tell me about this ship and who is investing." His father sat back to wait.

"The ship is called, *The Abigail*. It is captained by a well-respected man, Thomas MacFarland, who is recommended by Evan's father, Robert Macleod. He is who first brought it to our attention as a way to make money and recover from our…financial…destitution."

"Interesting." His father frowned. "Why is Robert Macleod not investing himself?"

"He has passed on the opportunity to help Evan."

"I see. Very well. I will consider loaning you the capital. If I do, you will repay with interest."

There was lightening in his chest to know that he could possibly have his portion of the money. He wasn't disappointed in the fact he'd not acquire the capital from seducing a woman. The wager had been fun in that moment, but now it mattered very little to him. His father trusted him and that was worth more to him than a bet.

"I also wish to repay you for all the gambling debts, even if it means keeping very little for myself."

His father's eyebrows rose. "Is that so?"

"It means more to me that you trust me than whatever profit comes from the ship."

When his father looked to the ledger in front of him, Henry cleared his throat. His father knew him well and looked up.

"Whatever it is, I cannot go against your mother's wishes. I agree with her that you must marry and soon."

"I am going to propose marriage to Hannah Kerr."

At the statement, if it was possible, his father's eyebrows shot up higher. "What?"

"I am in love with her and cannot abide the idea of marriage to anyone but her. Hannah is who I will marry."

His father stood and refilled his glass. He took a large gulp and swallowed. "I do not think this will make your mother happy. I agree that the lass is fetching and quite brave."

Henry continued. "I am aware there are many impediments. Believe me, Father, I understand. However, I cannot help what I feel."

"No." His father gave him a stern look. "I cannot approve of it, son. Her brother owns gambling dens and is a criminal. For all we know, he murdered her father. Then there's the matter of her mother going mad. The lass brings too much detriment to our family."

"In all fairness, no one is aware they are siblings. That her father was murdered is not her fault. Her mother, well, that is troublesome."

While his father paced, Henry lowered to a chair. It would take time, but he had to convince his father. It would take having his support in order to convince his mother to agree to the marriage.

Although a grown man who did not require his parents' permission to marry, going against their wishes would mean a harder life for Hannah. Not only that, but he did not wish to cause either of his parents social harm.

Society and their standing was of utmost importance to his parents, and therefore, Henry needed them to agree to the marriage. His mother would be the best person to set in motion how to best present Hannah to society.

"Your mother will never agree to it," his father finally said. "You must understand. It is her circumstance that is worrisome."

Henry stood. "Father. You have met her. What do you truly think about her as a person? Forget everything else."

"I like her," his father replied without hesitation. "I think she is a good match for you. Quite independent and despite being alone has the bearings of a very respectable young woman."

"Can you tell Mother that? Will you please help me in this? Together we can convince her."

Once again, his father looked down at the paperwork in front of him. "I am not sure it will work. I myself am not convinced that a marriage to her would be beneficial to you. There are many other factors to consider, Henry. You know very well the lass would never be fully accepted by our peers. Why would you subject her to the scrutiny of our social circles?"

"I must insist." Henry could not think of what else to say. Whether his parents agreed to it or not, he would marry Hannah. That they were not included in social gatherings would not affect him one way or the other. Hannah would not miss what she'd never been part of.

"I am going to speak to Mother now." Henry met his father's gaze. "With or without your support."

Together they went to the solarium where his mother sat reading. She looked up, scanning their faces. "Whatever it is, it must be serious."

"Henry has an announcement to make," his father said, lowering to sit next to his wife. "Do not fret, dear, it is not so bad."

"What is it, dear?" his mother asked.

"I have decided to marry," Henry replied. "I am to ask Hannah Kerr to be my wife."

When his mother closed her eyes, Henry knew it was to keep from blurting something she'd regret. She opened them and looked up to him. "I will never agree to such foolishness. Honestly, Henry, how can you even consider it?"

"I love her."

"What you are is infatuated. You've convinced yourself to be her champion and now think she cannot possibly live without you." His mother put the book aside and gripped her hands together. "I will not allow it."

Taking a moment to gather his thoughts, Henry lowered to a chair across from his parents. "She is a wonderful woman who will bring me and this family happiness. If you would only give yourself the opportunity to get to know her, you will agree. Father has met her."

Lady Campbell turned to her husband. "What have you said to Henry about this?"

"I-I agree that the lass is a good match for him personality wise. However, I have warned Henry that she will never fit into our social circles and would be an outcast. He should not subject her to it."

"You make it sound as if our friends are horrible," his mother remarked. "They are not."

"I did not imply it. However, they are not the most accepting of people."

Henry cleared his throat. "Based on your own reactions, I would say neither of you are accepting of anyone without some sort of pedigree."

With a sharp look, his mother huffed. "I know you well, Henry, and you will do whatever you have made your mind up to do. Whether it harms this family matters little to you."

"Where is everyone?" His sister appeared, helped by her husband. Upon seeing them, she tugged her arm away. "This looks like a serious conversation. What happened?" There was an eagerness in her expression. Alana loved dramatics. Although she preferred it to be about her, when not, she would take it in any sort of way.

It could not be worse timing.

"Your brother has decided to marry a woman who is cloaked in scandal."

Henry's mouth fell open. "Mother, really? What scandal?"

"Her father was murdered. He was probably involved in some sort of illicit activity."

"Oh, you mean John Kerr, the owner of the tea shop?" Alana exclaimed. "Horrible thing that you had to find the body." She gave Henry what could pass for sympathy if not for the slight smile.

"Aren't you supposed to be home, having a child or something?" Henry murmured under his breath.

"I heard that," his sister replied. "Hopefully soon by the way it's kicking in there. I needed to get fresh air. So tired of resting and spending time inside."

He didn't point out that by coming there, she was still indoors.

"We should have her for dinner," Alana said with a wide smile. "It will give you the opportunity to observe her, Mother. It could be she will feel so inadequate, she will not marry Henry."

"Absolutely not," Henry snapped. "I will not have her come here to be humiliated."

His mother remained silent, looking at him without expression.

"I did not say humiliate," his sister replied. "I mean it will give us the opportunity to get to know her. Marriage is a big step." She turned to her husband who ran around trying to control the other three children. "Isn't that right, dear?"

"What?" He lifted a child and sniffed its bottom. "Oh yes, of course."

As a nanny appeared to take the children away, his mother watched and then turned to him. "I think it is a good idea. Bring her to dinner tonight."

"Tonight?"

"Yes, the sooner the better. I wish to meet this woman who has turned your head."

"TONIGHT?" HANNAH STARED at him, aghast. "Why?"

They sat in the parlor that was alight with sunlight and fresh air as she'd left the French doors open to the weather.

"My mother wishes to meet you." Henry wondered how much to divulge. His sister had decided to remain, therefore, Hannah would be facing both Campbell women.

Hannah searched his face as if he held the answers to what she should do. "What did you tell them?"

"That I was in love with you and wish to marry you."

As he spoke, her eyes grew wider and wider.

"You did what?" Her hands flew to her cheeks, and she blew out a breath. "Why would you tell them that?"

"Because it is the truth."

She looked beautiful that day. When he'd arrived, she'd been in the parlor that had been redecorated with a small table and chairs. A newly hired maid was placing vases of fresh flowers on the table and sideboard.

"Henry we cannot possibly. Surely your mother and father are against it. Besides…" she reached for his face, cupped his jaw, and looked into his eyes. "You have not asked me, and I have not accepted."

There was a tightening in his stomach. It was true, he'd taken for granted that she would marry him once he asked. It was presumptuous of him.

"Do you love me?"

The words hung in the air. Hannah let out a long sigh and met his gaze again. "You know I do."

"If I know anything about you, it is that you are one of the bravest women I have ever known. You have faced what life has thrown at you with dignity and strength. Fight with me for our love, Hannah."

She bowed her head.

Lowering to one knee before her, Henry took her hands. "Hannah Kerr, will you do me the honor of becoming my wife?"

"I find that I cannot say no." Her eyes glistened with unshed tears. "I will. Yes. Oh Henry, what are we doing?"

He stood and brought her into his arms, holding her close as he tried to keep from allowing the most unmasculine of emotions free rein.

"We must tell our friends," Hannah said after a few moments in which they sat quietly, both needing a moment to become used to the idea.

"We should." He agreed, happiness bubbling inside him.

Hannah looked at him. "Are we compatible? What do we possibly have in common?"

As expected, an intelligent woman like Hannah would delve into reasoning.

"I believe we are very compatible."

"In what ways?" She took his left hand in hers. "Tell me."

"Attracted to one another. We are good friends. I enjoy our time together whether we sit in silence or have a conversation."

Hannah nodded. "True. I suppose people with much less

marry and have a good marriage."

"What else can you think of?" Henry prodded, knowing she had to be fully convinced in order for them to move forward.

"Do you like opera?" she asked.

"No."

She giggled. "I do not care for it either. What about dogs?" Hannah looked to her newly acquired pet who slept soundly on a bed made of a folded blanket.

"Yes, I do. I also like cats."

"Really?" Hannah studied him. "What about...?" She stopped and smiled at him. "I cannot fathom life without you. Each day that we are apart, I miss you terribly."

"That is exactly how I feel. If that is not compatibility, I do not know what is." Henry pressed a kiss to her temple.

Marta appeared at the doorway. "Tea?"

"Yes, please." Hannah stood and went to her housekeeper. "Mister Campbell has asked me to marry him, and I have accepted." Her face turned a delightful shade of pink.

The housekeeper looked past her employer to Henry. "I certainly hope so. There has been too much familiarity between you. I know it is not my place to say so, but I was going to speak to you privately, Mister Campbell, and express my concern and ask that you marry this wonderful young woman soon."

Henry closed the distance and met the woman's gaze. "You would have been very right to do so." He pressed a kiss to the startled woman's cheek. "Thank you."

The woman rushed to hug Hannah, her eyes bright. "I am so very delighted for you, Miss Hannah."

When the women began crying, Henry quickly made himself useful, handing Hannah his handkerchief and Marta one he spotted on a side table.

Then he poured three glasses of brandy and, in between sniffles, they toasted to the engagement.

UPON ARRIVING AT the Macleod home, they found the young couple in the parlor. It seemed as if they were having a disagreement by the lack of expression upon their entrance.

Felicity met Hannah's gaze. "What happened? Is something wrong? You look as if you've cried."

"I did a bit," Hannah admitted. "We have news."

Evan came and stood next to Felicity. "Come sit down, please." He looked past them to the butler. "Pour some wine, please."

Unsure if it should be him to tell them, Henry looked to Hannah, who seemed to be on the verge of tears again.

"Please tell me. What happened?" Felicity insisted, hurrying to Hannah and placing an arm around her shoulders.

Henry smiled. "Hannah has accepted my proposal of marriage."

When Felicity screamed with excitement, her companion, Ana, and the butler hurried over; they stopped in the doorway at seeing Hannah and Felicity embraced and jumping up and down while laughing.

Evan came to him hand outstretched. "I knew it." He gave him a knowing look. "It was only a matter of time before you admitted how you felt to yourself."

"Congratulations!" Felicity rushed to him and threw her arms around his waist. "I am so very happy."

They toasted to the engagement, the entire time Hannah looking at him with so much love that his heart melted. She expected him to be her strength, to defend her and protect her always, and he would.

Once they toasted, he and Evan were pushed aside, the women going to the opposite side of the room to discuss matters that they deemed them not needed for.

"We are expected at my parents' home this evening. Do not

forget," Henry said to Hannah who looked over and nodded.

"How do you expect that to go?" Evan asked.

"Honestly, I do not know. Father likes Hannah and I am sure my sister will adore her. Mother on the other hand worries more about the social repercussions than whether or not we are in love. As you can imagine, if she does not approve, Father will follow suit."

They waited a few moments, Evan looking over to the women, who were engrossed in conversation. Hannah seemed to be retelling how the proposal happened.

"What about the sponsorship?"

Henry shook his head. "I am not sure. Father is considering loaning me the rest of what I need. However, this may dampen his will to do so. If he uses the fact I am marrying Hannah as a way to not loan me the money, I will have to consider something else."

"Like what?"

"I have an investment I have not considered. A wager, of sorts."

Evan looked surprised. "Is it something that could be dangerous? Or unscrupulous?"

"I won a bet five years ago. I never collected upon it."

Seeming to understand whatever was to be said had to be between them, Evan stood. "Let us go to my study."

THE FOG WAS thick, making it impossible to see even one foot in front of the other. Henry stumbled from the doorway, pulling his cape tight around his body. He'd won a great deal of money, and yet had left empty-handed. The only evidence of his winnings was a rapidly scribbled note.

That it had cost a man's life made the entire event surreal. Why had he entered into such a game? He'd succumbed so deep into his addiction to gambling that he was willing to wager his life against another. The idea of it, the disgust in himself, grew with each step he took.

After a few steps, he went to the side of a building and threw up. The smell of blood lingering in his nostrils despite the distance he put between him and the gambling den.

The instructions were to take the note to the bank and ask for Mister Billings. The money would be held in his name in a safety deposit box. All he had to do was collect it whenever he wished.

EVAN BLEW OUT a breath. "I didn't know it had become so bad."

"It was the last time I gambled." Henry stared into the glass in his hand. "I could never touch the money. A man died for it. All because of a bad hand."

"Did you kill him?" Evan met his gaze. It was obvious that no matter the reply, his friend would stand by him. There was nothing that could be done at this juncture as he had no idea who his opponent was.

"No. Someone stood behind each of the players. The last two who remained wagered life. We could fold at any moment. When I saw my hand and knew it was virtually unbeatable, I almost did. Just so the man would not die. But the man behind me nudged me and I realized he saw my hand and would not allow it. If I didn't show my hand, I would be the one to die."

"How?"

"Cutting of the throat."

"Fast and painless," Evan said. "Still a steep price."

Henry drank the last of his brandy. "I tried to find out who he was. When I returned to the place where he'd played, it had been abandoned. I wanted to give his family the money."

"If you use the money for your portion, would you feel badly about it?"

"I don't know anymore. I suppose there is nothing that can be done about it now. I could give it away to a charitable cause."

Evan met his gaze. "I think you should take the amount you

need. Upon the ship returning and us making our profit, replace it. Leave it there until you figure out what to do with it."

"A man died..."

"You wagered your life as well. Both of you were idiots. You won the money fairly. One of you had to die that day. Guilt does not change the truth of the matter."

Henry laughed. "You sound like your father."

When Evan groaned, they both laughed. It felt good to share the burden he'd carried for so long.

CHAPTER THIRTEEN

"I HAVE TO wear a suitable color. I am barely out of mourning," Hannah said while sitting in Felicity's room.

Henry had gone home, and she would go by carriage later. They'd decided that Felicity was to accompany her, for which she was eternally grateful.

Now in her friend's bedchamber, they went through Felicity's wardrobe trying to decide what was best to wear.

"What about this?" Felicity held out a beautiful gray ensemble. The gown was soft and downy with tiny pink rosebuds embroidered around the neckline and hem of the sleeves.

"It's beautiful."

"Wear it. You can have it," Felicity said with a smile. "I find that whenever I try it on, I never choose to wear it."

While Ana, Felicity's personal maid, combed Hannah's hair, she met Felicity's gaze in the mirror. "I am not sure what to expect. Tell me about Missus Campbell."

Her friend bit her bottom lip in thought. "She is attractive. Favors the color blue. From the few times I have been in the same socials with her, she seems to be well-liked. Has a close-knit group of women whom she spends time with doing various charity events and such."

"Have you ever had a conversation with her?" Hannah wanted to know everything about the woman.

"Nothing more than pleasantries," Felicity replied. "I wish Mother were here. She knows her a bit better than I do. I believe

Mother has been to their house several times."

"What about the dance? How was she acting?"

"She was in her element. The music, décor, and food were extravagant. It was obvious she'd spent a great deal of time planning every detail. According to my mother, it is what she loves to do."

"I see," Hannah said. "She and your mother have that in common."

It seemed too soon before it was time to go. As they descended the stairs, Evan gave her an approving look. "You will win them over. I have no doubt."

Hannah blinked away grateful tears. "I certainly hope you are right."

Once assisted into the carriage, they set off for the Campbell estate, which was not far from where Felicity lived. At the most, it would take half an hour for them to arrive.

She'd ridden past the Campbell estate many times, always admiring the decorative gates with the family crest. Now as the carriage went through them, Hannah felt as if she was about to be sick.

Felicity took her hand. "You're pale."

"I am not sure I can go through with this. They will never accept me. I am sure of it."

Nothing else was said. Probably because there wasn't anything that Felicity could say that would help her feel any better.

The house was alight, every window bright and welcoming. If not for the huge boulder in her stomach, Hannah would have thought they were glad for her visit.

There was another carriage and they waited for whoever it was to be seen to. When their carriage rolled forward, Hannah gasped audibly. She bowed her head. "Lord help me."

"I am sure it is not as bad as that," Felicity said, but there was a slight tremble to her voice.

Henry came to greet them, holding her hand as she descended. "How are you?" he asked, a slight curve to his lips.

Hannah could not speak; she managed a smile in reply.

Looking to the other carriage, Henry shook his head. "My sister Alana is here. She is heavy with child and should be home in bed."

"Oh." It was the only word Hannah could conjure in that moment.

Felicity came to his side. "We may as well go inside."

They went up the steps, each of them on Henry's arm. Upon arriving at the entry, they were greeted by a butler who took their wraps.

She was much too nervous to notice more than the extravagant flower arrangement in the foyer as they went to a sitting room where several people gathered and were talking.

At their entrance, everyone turned to them.

"Mother, Father, Sister, may I introduce Miss Hannah Kerr." Henry's voice was steady. He turned to Hannah and walked with her to where his parents sat. "You already know my father."

Hannah nodded and did a quick slight curtsey.

"This is Catriona Campbell, my mother."

Hannah kept her gaze lowered, head bent as she lowered to a curtsey. "I am very pleased to make your acquaintance."

Henry didn't wait and motioned to the other woman in the room. "My sister, Alana Robertson."

Once again, Hannah curtsied, fully aware that Henry's mother studied her.

Henry escorted her to sit and then brought Felicity into the room. "You have all met Missus Felicity Macleod. She agreed to attend as Hannah's companion."

"You have no one else then?" Lady Campbell asked, her eyes pinning her. "A companion?"

"I am alone," Hannah replied. "I do have a woman in my employ, Marta, who accompanies me whenever I leave the house."

The woman slid a look to Felicity. "How is your mother, Felicity?"

"Very well, thank you for asking," Felicity replied.

Henry's sister was indeed quite late with child. She seemed uncomfortable by the way she leaned back in the chair. Hannah met her gaze. "How much longer?"

Seeming pleased to be spoken to, Alana grimaced. "Another month at least." She let out a sigh. "Everything hurts."

"Ah yes, drinks," Lord Campbell said with much enthusiasm. "Welcome to our home, Miss Kerr."

Alana seemed to sink further into the chair, her feet barely touching the floor.

Unable to stand it, Hannah looked to Lady Campbell. "May I use one of the pillows to make her more comfortable?"

"I doubt anything can make Alana more comfortable."

Felicity and Hannah exchanged looks and stood. While Hannah placed a pillow behind Alana's back, Felicity slid a footstool under her swollen feet.

"Oh my goodness, I could weep. This is perfect," Alana exclaimed, her hands crossed over her extended stomach. "You must show my lady how to do it."

"Hannah and Felicity volunteer at the woman's maternity ward in the city," Henry told his parents.

Mrs. Campbell frowned. "I am not sure an unmarried woman should be exposed to such things."

"There is great need and not enough workers to help," Felicity replied with a smile. "They are very careful when assigning duties."

Instead of a reply, Mrs. Campbell slid a look at her daughter. "You should be home, Alana. I do not understand why you are traipsing all over town in your state."

A young female servant came to the door to announce that dinner was ready.

No one moved. It was as if everyone waited for something. Hannah wasn't sure, so she looked at Henry who in turn gave his parents a bland look.

"A word, Hannah," Mrs. Campbell said, and then looked to

Felicity, Henry, and her daughter who seemed to have fallen asleep. "In private."

Giving his mother what seemed like a warning look, he held out his arm to Felicity and escorted her out of the room.

"Do not dawdle," his father said as he went to Alana, who refused to budge, murmuring something about resting for the first time. Hannah wondered if she just wanted to be nosy and hear whatever her mother was about to say.

Hannah lifted her gaze to the woman. It was obvious that both Henry and Alana, who was lovely, got their good looks from their mother. Although older, Catriona Campbell remained a beauty.

Lips pursed as if considering what to say, she studied Hannah for a long moment.

It took all her will not to speak first and tell the woman she cared very little about society and all the rules that her marriage with Henry would violate.

"My son is quite taken with you."

Hannah nodded.

"I can see why. You are a lovely young thing."

"Thank you."

The woman looked to the doorway. "I suppose there is no need to explain to you why a marriage between you would be detrimental to Henry's status in the community. It would bring scandal to our doorstep. Surely you do not want that."

"Scandal is everywhere, Mrs. Campbell. I am not sure what scandal you speak of. That my father was murdered was neither his fault nor mine. Once the killer is brought to justice, you will learn it had nothing to do with any type of felonious undertaking on his part."

The woman seemed taken aback by her long response. "You seem very sure about it."

"I know my father was a respectable man, a man with unwavering values. He would never be part of anything criminal. I have done investigating of my own."

Mrs. Campbell's face hardened. "And so have I. Perhaps not your father, but your mother has a rather questionable past. It will come to light. If you marry my son, one of the most eligible men in Glasgow, inquiries will be made." She held out a hand. "And before you say it isn't true. I know our social circles. They are not keen to accept an unknown woman, without any kind of credentials to recommend her, readily."

"Mother!" Alana fought to sit up. "You are being cruel."

"I am being honest. This lass has to know what she is facing. What Henry will have to endure."

Hannah stood. She wanted to run from the room and straight out the door. However, if she were to be honest, she'd not expected a warm welcome.

"If your circles are such as you describe, why would anyone wish to be part of them? I prefer true friendships to horrible people who cannot see past a person's personal worth."

"We cannot change society," Mrs. Campbell replied, her tone clipped. "It is the way of the world."

"Perhaps," Hannah replied. "But we can change whom we surround ourselves with."

She stood and walked to the doorway, fully aware it was rude to not wait for the matriarch. Once in the hallway, she listened for voices and then entered the dining room.

At once, Henry stood and came to greet her. He searched her face, but she'd already schooled it. "This is such a beautiful room."

"Err…yes. It is." He ushered her to a chair and assisted her to sit.

His mother and Alana entered after and were seated. Both looked to Hannah, who sipped her wine wishing it were something stronger. She refused to look at Felicity, as her friend would immediately know she was furious.

"I am glad for everyone to be here. Let us raise a glass to Henry and Hannah," Henry's father, bless him, tried to lighten the mood in the room.

Everyone lifted their glasses and took a sip.

Henry then cleared his throat. "I would like to toast Hannah. For her bravery in coming here and accepting to marry me despite the obstacles that will present themselves. I am proud of you." When he met her gaze and winked, Hannah smiled. Only Henry could lighten her mood with but a look.

His mother exchanged looks with Alana, who seemed delighted at what had to be the most drama she'd experienced in months.

The meal looked delicious; however, to Hannah, it tasted horrible. Either it was bland, or the conversation with Henry's mother had left a bitter taste in her mouth.

Thankfully, Felicity kept the conversation going, bringing up the butterfly ball and the upcoming women's tea at her house.

"I will ensure an invitation is delivered promptly," Felicity said and then looked to Alana. "I suppose you will not be able to attend."

Alana grimaced. "No sadly."

Henry's father met Hannah's gaze. "What about you, sweet girl. Do you plan to begin hosting soon?"

"I am currently redecorating. But once it is completed, I hope to host ladies for tea."

"Will there be someone living with you that can chaperone?" Mrs. Campbell asked. She knew full well what her situation was.

"Mrs. Murray has agreed to chaperone once I host events. I am still awaiting word from my aunt. I've invited her to live with me."

Alana frowned. "Where is your mother?"

When Hannah took a breath, Henry spoke. "After Hannah's father was killed, her mother felt a calling to join the convent."

"For propriety's sake, I would think she could ignore the calling until her daughter was established." Mrs. Campbell shook her head. "Why would she leave?"

Henry's father's eyes shined with interest at the turn in the conversation. Hannah exchanged worried looks with Felicity.

Her friend attempted to intervene. "She was not strong enough to handle the death and did not take it well."

"Not the time for this discussion. There is naught that can be done now," Henry added.

Alana's forlorn expression, as if on the brink of tears, was strange. "You poor dear. I cannot imagine going through so much." She slid a look to her mother. "We should all strive to be kind to Hannah."

"There is no need to warn us about such things, Alana," Mr. Campbell said, looking to both his wife and daughter. "I think they have enough to face. We should support them."

Hannah adored the man in that moment.

Mrs. Campbell straightened. "A mother ensures that her children do well and have the best of everything. No one can blame me for wishing that Henry make a wise decision and marry the right person."

"That is what I am doing, Mother," Henry replied. "I do not require the approval of anyone but the people in this room."

"Our social circles…our acquaintances…" Mrs. Campbell made circular motions with her hands. "What about their reactions? You cannot pretend to be completely immune. What about me and your father?"

"Calm down, dear. I am sure things will work themselves out."

For a beat, everyone was silent. Hannah wasn't sure what she felt. On one hand, she would not break Henry's heart, or hers for that matter, because of what Mrs. Campbell suggested. On the other hand, she worried that the woman was right. It would not affect her, the marriage, but what exactly would be the impact on Henry's family?

"I am not sure who all you refer to, Mrs. Campbell," Felicity said. "If you remember correctly, Lord Thomas married a woman who's been divorced twice. The Duke of Stallings left his wife and is now living in Edinburgh with a woman half his age. His wife, the duchess, keeps lovers and is not discreet about it. Then there is the latest scandal, Felicity Murray marrying the rogue, Evan Macleod." She took a breath and looked to Hannah. "The only thing that my dear friend Hannah will bring to your family is her strength, bravery, and deep abiding love for your Henry."

A tear trickled down Hannah's cheek. Never had she felt so supported and loved as she did in that moment. Henry took her hand and squeezed it.

"I am in total agreement with Felicity. With your outward support of our marriage, it will stop some of the gossips who will be too afraid to lose your esteem," Henry added.

After dinner, the men remained in the dining room and the women returned to the parlor, where the subject was changed to a more neutral topic of the weather and gardening.

Finally, it neared time to leave.

"Thank you very much for a lovely meal," Hannah said to Mrs. Campbell. "I am sorry you are upset. I hope one day, you will come to accept me."

The woman let out a breath. "My sentiments have nothing to do with you. You are a lovely young woman." She turned to Felicity. "I will ponder on what you have said."

On the carriage ride home, Felicity went on about how horrible Mrs. Campbell had been to Hannah. "I expected more from her. I've always thought her to be a nice person."

"She is a product of her upbringing. People of the aristocracy are brought up to think of nothing more than social standing and what others think," Hannah said. "I understand her wishing for a good match for Henry."

"Nonetheless. Henry has chosen you. She will have to accept it." Felicity gave her a stern look. "And don't you get it into your head that anything she said is valid."

Hannah giggled. "I certainly was having second thoughts. Until your speech."

Both laughed.

There would be interesting days ahead. Hannah prayed it would not change things between her and Henry.

CHAPTER FOURTEEN

IT FELT LIKE old times when Henry arrived at Evan's home and found his three friends lounging in the parlor.

Evan sat at the piano, slow notes of nothing familiar filling the air. Miles sat on a chair, his long legs stretched out as he studied the liquid in his glass.

Then there was Grant, who he'd not expected to be there. Felicity's brother stood next to the sideboard pouring brandy into two glasses.

"I see you have returned and look well," Henry said, crossing the room and taking one of the glasses. "What news do you bring from abroad?"

"He has not said a word as of yet," Miles said, his deep voice with tones of boredom. "I expect he waited on your arrival."

The music stopped and Evan studied them. "So far it seems only I have come up with the money. Admittedly not quite as planned. We have but eight weeks before I have to meet with Captain MacFarland."

"I will have the money shortly," Grant said with a smirk. "She's agreed to gift it to me, despite my insistence to repay it."

"Ha," Miles barked out. "I doubt you put much effort into the argument."

"It doesn't matter." Grant lowered to a chair. "I will have my portion." He looked to Henry. "What about you?"

"Not sure," Henry replied with honesty. "There is a chance I will not have it. I have asked my father for a loan, and he is considering it. Then there is another way that I am considering."

Evan huffed. "Henry will have the money. Miles?"

Lord Johnstone lifted his glass and studied it. "It seems that the only one who has so far stuck to the rules of how to come up with the money is Grant. Therefore, I will do you one better." He looked at Grant. "I will pursue, seduce, and get the money from a woman in one week. I will wait until it is almost time and then I will begin my pursuit."

"Very sure of your abilities for someone whose plans just fell through," Henry said with a laugh.

Of course Miles could afford to take such chances in order to beat Grant. He was wealthy and if worse came to worse and he could not acquire the money by seducing an affluent woman, he could pay it himself.

Evan stood and went to the doors, pulling them closed. "Tell us about this woman, Grant."

They waited as Grant refilled his already empty glass. "Not much to tell. I will admit to never knowing someone so extremely rich. We traveled throughout Europe staying in ostentatious mansions and estates that rivaled the Versailles. The banquets and balls that we attended had to have cost a king's ransom. At times, I had to go for long walks so as to not fall into the spell of thinking I belonged. Although the degree of luxury can be quite attractive, it was all so very... contrived." He continued, "Everyone spent most days sitting about espousing about the stupidest things. The imports of fabrics, the lack of taste of whatever delicacy they'd eaten the day before. Every little thing was nitpicked because they had nothing else to do. Then after tea, everyone would go to their perspective spaces and spend hours preparing for whatever evening fete they chose to attend."

Grant emptied his cup. "There was some kind of social, must-be-attended gathering every single night." He looked at each of them. "Every. Single. Night."

While he took a breath, Henry, Miles, and Evan exchanged amused looks.

"How much longer will this continue?" Henry asked. "You cannot very well walk off into the sunset once you have the money in hand."

The butler appeared and refilled the decanter with more brandy, his gaze moving about the room. "Would you like something to eat in here, sir?" he asked Evan, who nodded.

"That is certainly something I have to consider," Grant replied with a pensive expression. "How long can I withstand it?"

Listening to Grant gave Henry a short reprieve. He'd expected to be questioned upon entering about the engagement. To his surprise, his friends either didn't know, or did not consider it interesting.

"What?" Henry asked, noting everyone looking to him. So much for the reprieve.

"I asked why you have not come up with the money, but instead have to ask for a loan from your father?" Miles asked. "You had planned to marry a young unsuspecting lady with a huge dowry. Had you not?"

It was his turn to make an announcement. Although Evan already knew, he'd left it to him to announce.

"I am engaged to Hannah Kerr. Although she has come about an inheritance of sorts, it is not enough for my portion. Therefore, I have failed in my quest to marry wealth."

Both Evan and Grant were quick to congratulate him. Each of them nearing and hugging him with enthusiasm and wide smiles.

By the study of him by Miles, Henry expected his aristocratic friend was not as enthused with the idea.

"I am going to marry her, Miles. My parents are informed, albeit not happy about it." Henry held out his hand. "Are you not going to congratulate me?"

Instead of taking his hand right away, Miles stood to his full towering height and then shook it. "Have you thought this through? There is the matter of Jules Brown and his unsavory business. It could…no, it will cause problems."

"I have taken it all into consideration. There is nothing Jules

Brown can do that would affect my family or my marriage. It was obvious he wished nothing to do with Hannah other than to acquire that box."

Henry met Miles's gaze. "I understand your perspective. It is not lost on me that if things were different, it would be simpler to marry someone from our social circles. However, I have made up my mind."

"Will you marry someone of your class just to ensure to keep the right pedigree in your family?" Grant asked with a lazy grin directed at Miles.

"I would rather not marry than risk harm," Miles replied. He turned his attention back to Henry. "We can try to ignore things, and for the most part, I prefer not to think of titles and such. However, it is inescapable. There are certain responsibilities that cannot be ignored. You will be quite wealthy upon your father's death."

Picturing punching Miles was easier than listening to yet another person explain the responsibilities of their social standing. It was ridiculous.

"Do you hear yourself?" Henry finally said. "Lecturing me as if I was just born yesterday. I come from a long lineage. Clan Campbell was and continues to be the most powerful presence in Scotland. I do not take my duties lightly. Hannah Kerr has every quality desired in a lady; she will not waver in her duties. I have little doubt of her abilities. Therefore, the only obstacle is people who think that all begins and ends within the ridiculous clutch we live in."

"I do wish you the best," Miles said. "I really do." His friend frowned. "I wish it were different. I am only presenting the facts, not how I personally believe."

Henry relented. "I understand your concerns and do know you are not an elitist. I hope that when you fall in love, she will be your social equal. It is much easier that way."

"I will support you in this," Miles assured him. Both Evan and Grant repeated that they'd help wherever they could.

Once again, Evan began playing the piano, the music soft and a bit melancholy.

"Should we visit this Jules Brown and ensure he will not be a problem for Hannah?" Grant asked.

Despite the fact Henry had considered the same thing, he shook his head. "It is probably best we let things as they are. It cannot be a good idea."

Evan stopped playing. "You should be receiving invitations. Felicity and I are hosting a gathering, nothing elaborate. She is itching to introduce Hannah properly to those who will be more amenable to your marriage."

UPON ENTERING HANNAH'S house, Henry immediately sensed something was wrong. Hannah did not stand to greet him upon him entering the parlor. Instead, she looked up at him with a worried expression.

"Is something wrong?" Henry looked to Hannah and then to Marta, who lingered at the door.

When Hannah did not reply, Marta let out a long sigh. "Your mother sent a letter."

It was then he noticed the crumpled paper clutched in Hannah's hand. She took a shaky breath and held it up to him. "We will not marry, Henry. Your family will never accept me. I cannot possibly do that to you. Please leave."

His heart thundered in his chest as he read the words. His mother's attempt to dissuade Hannah by informing her that he'd be outcast by his family and society for marrying someone whose brother owned gambling dens.

"Who told her?" Hannah asked.

Henry sighed. "Probably my father. He can never keep secrets from her. I am sure it was a slip and not intentional."

"For the best," Hannah said, sounding tired. "That she knows everything. We should have told her. It was bound to come out sooner or later."

He lowered to sit next to Hannah and took her hand. Marta walked away to give them privacy, although Henry was sure she remained within earshot.

"I will not be outcast from my family. My mother is shocked at the news and thinking the worst will happen. I ask that you give me a few days to smooth things over. Once I explain that Jules will never be part of your life…"

"Won't he?" Hannah interrupted. "How do we know this? He is my half-brother, and not only that, but I do wish to know if he killed my father. There are too many issues, Henry. Please understand me. I cannot marry you and go into our marriage with so many unanswered questions and obstacles in the way."

Unable to keep from it, Henry released her hand and stood. "Is that how little you care for me? That you allow exterior things to compromise what we have?"

Hannah took a fortifying breath. "It is because of how dear you are to me that I wish to keep you and your family away from everything that a marriage to me brings. Understand me."

"I do understand. You should also see my view of things. It matters not to me if you bring an entire army of adversaries. I would fight every single one for you. For us."

"I am not that strong."

"Then there is little to be said." Henry stormed from the room, too angry to remain civil. He knew exactly where he needed to go.

JULES BROWN SAT across from Henry, his gaze pinning him as he considered the questions he'd asked.

"If I am to be honest."

"I would expect it," Henry countered.

Jules's eyes narrowed. "If I am to be completely honest, I have not decided whether or not I will speak to Hannah again. She believes me to be a murderer. To have killed her father."

"Or paid someone to do it."

"My father's dying wish was to find the box. He told me to question John Kerr."

"Your father died years ago. Why did you wait?"

Jules looked away. "Because I didn't consider it important. I was not close to my father. However, I had to find out where the box was. I made a promise."

After a hesitation, he continued. "I did send someone to question Mr. Kerr. When I found out he'd killed him, I had the killer… dispatched. After Mr. Kerr died, I sent someone to question Mrs. Kerr about it."

Now it made sense why Hannah's mother had left so suddenly. It could be that in her own way, she'd hoped to distract the men away from Glasgow.

"Why would you want to continue any contact with Hannah? I can relay the information to her." Henry cleared his throat. "I have asked Hannah to marry me, and she had accepted. However, now she is worried that any affiliation with you would cause damage, socially, to my family. She broke it off. However, I am fighting to remove any reason for her to not marry me."

The man's gaze fell and when he lifted it to Henry, there was anger. "And you come to me and ask that I stay away. I am a blemish."

"After what you've told me, how can I not have a negative opinion of you? Your profession alone is harmful to Hannah."

Jules stood, poured whiskey into a pair of glasses, and offered Henry one, which he took.

"I will visit my sister one time. To explain the circumstances of her father's death. After, I will never speak to her again."

"If I know her, she will want a relationship with you," Henry admitted. "I do wish things were different."

"If my…sister is anything like me, she will find a way to make things work."

In his heart, Henry realized the siblings were alike. Hannah had decided the best way forward was for the marriage to be canceled. To continue life without him.

"I believe you and she will find you do have a great deal in common."

Under different circumstances, Henry would have liked the man. However, whether or not he accepted it, he'd had John Kerr killed. And surely there were gamblers who continued to be harmed for not paying debts. A man who owned gambling dens was never without being part of wrongdoing.

"I hope you understand why I had to come." Henry placed his glass down and stood. "I want to protect Hannah."

Jules nodded. There was nothing else to be said.

WHEN HE ARRIVED home late that evening, his mother and father were in the solarium having tea. He walked into the room and sat across from them. "Hannah broke off our engagement."

His parents exchanged looks.

"You should not have sent that letter," his father said to his mother. "The poor girl is probably heartbroken."

Of course his mother would not waver on her stance. "It is for the best. You will see." She reached for his hand, but Henry moved it. "Darling. There are so many beautiful women. It will be a bit, but you will find that Hannah was not the one for you."

"I am moving, I have purchased a townhome in the city," Henry announced. "Father, I no longer require the loan."

His mother was first to react, eyes widening and hand over her chest. "You cannot move out. What purpose will it serve?"

"Additionally," Henry said, "I relinquish my inheritance. I will not be taking over responsibilities of the Campbell fortune." He looked to his father. "Please pass it to Alana's eldest."

With that, he stood and went up the stairs to his bedroom.

At once, his valet entered. "Sir?"

"Pack up everything. I am moving to the city. Ensure you do not leave one single thing I own. All the clothes, personal belongings, and bedding." He glanced around to take in everything in the room. He went to the small sitting room next to it. "Pack my books."

He then pulled out a large bag and began packing what he'd need for a few days.

"When shall this be taken? Can I come with you?"

Henry considered his resources. After purchasing the townhouse and paying his portion of the payment for the ship, he had enough to live comfortably until the ship returned.

"Yes you may. Your pay will remain the same for the time being, however."

When he returned to the first floor, his father called out. "Henry."

He dropped his bags and went to the doorway that led to his father's study. "What is it, Father?"

"Will you continue to work with me? I do need you to continue to oversee things. Even if you insist on relinquishing your inheritance. You will remain responsible for your mother if something happens to me."

Henry nodded. "Of course, I am not shirking my responsibilities."

"We will meet at least twice a week, here." His father left no room for argument.

"Father," Henry began. "You did not seem surprised at my announcement."

His father's lips curved. "I had deduced what would happen upon your mother sending that missive. You reacted as I would have expected." His father chuckled. "Your mother is quite upset. Give her time."

"The damage is done. Hannah has called off the engagement."

His father gave him a surprised look. "What are you going to do about it? A Campbell does not give up. A Campbell takes charge."

CHAPTER FIFTEEN

As much as Hannah appreciated Felicity's attempt to distract her by taking her to dinner at the Murrays' home, she really wanted to go home and be alone.

The lively conversation around the room was almost grating. Admittedly, it was nice to see Grant was in attendance although there was little interaction with his father.

"All those social events sound exhausting," Mrs. Murray exclaimed. "I cannot say I envy the life of the very rich."

Grant turned to Hannah. "Henry told me you and he are to marry. I am very happy for you."

There was a stony silence. It seemed everyone except for Grant was aware the engagement had been called off.

"I have decided not to accept his proposal after all." Hannah let out a breath and attempted at a smile. "It was a beautiful dream, but there are too many obstacles."

"Ah," Grant remarked. "Like my sister, I always considered you to be a bit of a rebel. I suppose you must have not felt strongly enough if you are not fighting for him."

How dare a rogue like Grant accuse her of not loving Henry enough?

"I love Henry. Which is why I am willing to sacrifice myself to not affect him or his family negatively. You have been gone. Are not aware of my half-brother."

Grant waved away her words and Hannah fought not to throw her glass at his head.

"Social standings, scandals, blah, blah, blah. Those people love a scandal; they live for marriages like yours so they have something to say to each other over tea. Then when the next social scandal comes along, they move on and all but forget you."

Felicity gave her brother a sharp look. "What are your plans now that you've returned from this time abroad with wealthy people?"

At her pointed comment, Grant nodded. "I do not know. I have finished a novel and will be meeting with a publisher in Edinburgh."

"A book?" Mr. Murray took in his son. "Do you not have better things to do. Like perhaps a proper occupation?"

The Murrays began debating what Grant should do while he smiled as if keeping a secret. Hannah decided he'd come up with his portion of the sponsorship capital and would soon be wealthy enough to do whatever he wished.

Hannah was grateful when she returned to her quiet and admittedly lonely house. The new maid greeted her and brought tea to her bedroom. Since Henry left, she'd not had a moment alone. It felt as if her world ended and she was now living a different reality.

She was too stunned for tears; there was no need for them. Crying meant that she still had emotions, but instead, there was an emptiness so vast every bit of her being was parched.

Movement outside the window caught her attention and she turned to the doorway. Had she left Betty outside? The poor thing would be terrified as she usually only stayed out as long as someone watched over her.

Hurrying down the stairs, Hannah went to the parlor and out the French doors. "Betty," she whispered. "Come here, girl."

There was nothing, no sound except for the wind.

"You have made this much easier." A figure appeared from the side of the house. "I planned to get a ladder and climb up to your window."

Hannah clasped a hand over her mouth to keep from shrieking. "Henry. What are you doing here? It is almost midnight."

"I have a plan. Whether you are willing or not, I will go through with it."

Dressed from head to toe in black, he looked every bit a villain. He wore a scarf that covered half his mouth and a cape that fell from his shoulders to his ankles.

"I thought my dog was outside. She's probably with Silas." Hannah gave her unexpected visitor what she hoped was a stern look. "There is nothing you can say that will change my mind."

He walked closer and she took a tentative step back. "I did not come to talk to you."

Hannah bit the inside of her cheek. Certainly she was dreaming. Henry went to the open French doors, threw something inside, and then hurried to where she stood still trying to make sense of what happened.

"Come along." He took her upper arm and guided her to the gates that led to the street. The gate was already open.

"What did you do?" Hannah peered out to the waiting carriage. "Who is in there?"

"Look and see," Henry replied cryptically.

She turned to face him. "I will not take another step unless you explain..." Everything went upside down as she was lifted and thrown over his shoulder.

"Put me down," Hannah hissed. "Someone will see."

Moments later, he plopped her none-to-gently onto the carriage seat and dropped next to her out of breath.

Hannah looked around in the dimness. There was no one else in the carriage, which immediately moved at a rather alarming speed.

"Are you cold?" Henry said, lifting a light blanket and attempting to put it over her shoulders. "I know you hadn't the opportunity to get a wrap."

Strange that in that moment, all Hannah could think was that Henry had lost his mind and she had to save him. She took a breath and turned to him.

"Henry, look at me."

When he did, it seemed that he was fully coherent. Then again, she had little experience with this sort of thing. Thinking back to when her mother had announced her departure, she'd seemed as if dazed. Henry did not look dazed.

"Have you been drinking?" Hannah asked then yelped and grabbed the edge of the seat when the carriage took a rather sharp turn.

"I have not. We are not going too far. A pair of hours."

"Where are we going?"

"You will see when we get there."

She hit his shoulder. "No I do not want to wait until I get there. It is the middle of the night. If we go somewhere for a pair of hours, by the time we return, it could be dawn."

"We are not returning right away." Henry sat back, crossed his arms, and closed his eyes. "Do not bother knocking on the roof. The driver has been instructed not to stop no matter what."

Hannah gawked at him, although it mattered little since he'd closed his eyes. "Why are you doing this?" When no reply came, she nudged him. "Henry? Answer me."

"It is best for you to rest and not worry. Everything will be clear in a bit."

For the next hour, she did her best to remain awake. But it was late, and she was emotionally drained. Finally, she gave up and leaned against the wall.

The sound of voices woke Hannah and she realized she was huddled against Henry, both of them covered in blankets.

She didn't dare open her eyes and face whoever spoke.

"We will be inside in a moment," Henry said to the person, who chuckled.

Whatever was happening was most peculiar. As annoyed as she was, it was with much reluctance that she pushed away from the warmth of Henry's body.

He gave her a sheepish smile. "We are here."

Obviously, he would not answer her questions, so Hannah

did the best she could to smooth her hair and then allowed him to help her from the carriage.

The moon gave enough light for her to see that they'd arrived at a small chapel. They hurried inside to find it alight with candles and a priest stood at the front. The driver and a monk walked in and stood near the front as well.

Hannah turned to Henry. "What are we doing here?"

"Isn't it obvious?" Henry replied. He took her hands. "Hannah, I love you with all my heart and am willing to give up all for you. Today, I relinquished my inheritance. I informed my parents that I was to marry you. I moved from their home and sent a messenger to come and inform my dear friend Father Bruce that I was to bring a woman and wished to get married this very night. Will you marry me?"

Something about his demeanor spoke volumes. Henry expected her to say no. Despite all he did, he knew her enough to know she was strong-willed and would not be bullied into making a hasty decision.

"Oh Henry," Hannah let out a long sigh. She looked to the other men in the chapel, who pretended not to listen. "This is the most unusual thing. It seems that nothing about my life is normal as of late."

It was not fair to him to not reply. It was evident he prepared for the worst.

Hannah reached up to touch his jaw. "You went to all this for me. How can I possibly say no? Yes. I will marry you."

With a loud laugh, Henry wrapped his arms around her and turned in a circle. "She said yes."

"What if she'd not agreed?" The priest shook his head. "I would've been cross to be up for this only to learn the lass wanted nothing to do with you."

THEY HELD HANDS while exchanging vows, the sounds of the wind outside the only accompaniment to the ceremony. At the same time, Hannah could not think of anything so romantic.

The candles' flickers played along the floors, walls, and faces of the five people gathered. Henry's soft gaze locked to hers as he professed to be faithful. Her voice shook when repeating the vows, a tear trailing down her cheek when they were pronounced husband and wife.

It wasn't until the priest pronounced them husband and wife and the other informed them a room had been prepared for them that Hannah finally felt as if it was all real.

She turned to Henry as they walked back out of the chapel to a small courtyard. "I cannot believe this. Marta will be horrified when waking and finding me gone."

"I left a message stating that you and I had gone to get married and to keep our secret."

Hannah wasn't sure what to say. "In the morning, I believe that I will be quite perturbed with you."

Instead of a reply, Henry gave her a devilish look.

The room they were shown was nicer than she expected. There was a four-poster bed, a washstand, and a wooden chest at the foot of the bed.

"Someone from the village will be here early and cook tomorrow," Father Bruce said. His gentle eyes met Hannah's. "I have known Henry since we were lads. He is a good man."

"He is," Hannah replied. "Thank you for staying up and doing all this for us."

The priest chuckled, and Hannah realized he was a rather handsome man. Much too handsome for a man of the cloth, in her opinion.

She smiled back. "Henry did not give me a choice."

When the door closed, every emotion she'd suppressed seemed to erupt. Arms extended she turned in a circle, face up, broad smile stretching. It was so freeing for some reason to do something so reckless. Her entire life had been changed in the span of the last two hours. Arguably, her entire existence had taken a turn the day her father died.

Tears streamed down her face as she came to a stop, and she rushed to the window to peer out into the darkness. "I cannot say I'm happy about how you went about this."

Seeming to understand she needed time, Henry stood back. It was such the way they'd gotten to know one another over the span of the last few months that he understood what she felt.

Hannah turned to face her new husband. "But I am so very glad you did it. If not, you and I would have allowed others to influence us and in the end, we would lose ourselves."

"I believe so, yes. However, it was my father who urged me to take control of things. Would I have otherwise? I am not sure."

It took a great deal of humility for him to admit it and yet by doing so, he grew in her estimation.

"Thank you for loving me enough." Henry neared. "For allowing me to spirit you away and marrying me. Thank you for being brave for the both of us."

Tears welled up in her eyes. "I love you Henry Aaron Campbell. As an added prize, I learned your middle name."

Both laughed.

"I already knew yours, Hannah Elizabeth," Henry quipped. "I once asked Felicity."

"You did?" It seemed a strange conversation to have at the moment when the bed loomed so large. Butterflies swooped and twirled in her stomach each time she glanced at it.

"Come." Henry took her hand and brought her closer to him. "Think of nothing but what is in the moment."

They kissed. It was a different sort of kiss, one of propriety almost. Hannah marveled in the knowledge that this man was her husband. That they would spend the rest of their lives together.

When his lips traveled from her lips down the side of her throat, she clung to him, wishing for the moment to never end.

The fabric of her dress seemed to take a life of its own as it slid down her shoulders and on past to land in a pool on the floor.

Henry lifted her from the pool at her feet and carried her to the bed. Then he placed her upon the bedding gently.

Never taking his gaze from hers, he undressed. First his jacket, then his shirt, exposing broad expanses of his body. When he undid the ties of his breeches, Hannah looked away, not prepared to see him fully undressed.

She heard the thumps of his boots and then the soft rustle of fabric. Finally, she dared to look at him, and the sight of Henry devoid of clothing caused her breath to catch.

It occurred to her in that moment that men were actually built like the statues from past centuries. Often she'd averted her gaze when inspecting one or the other, but every so often she'd pretended disinterest while studying the male body.

So now, as Henry climbed into the bed, she realized that he was indeed most perfectly formed.

"What are you thinking?"

A soft giggle escaped at the truth. "Would it insult you if I said your body is like the marble statues of times past?"

"I am about to make love to my wife for the first time and already she is comparing me to statues," Henry grumbled. "I do hope to be more lifelike." With a soft chuckle, he nibbled at her neck. "I pray to change your mind about me being a stone creation. Although I will admit being flattered that you believe me to be like a piece of art."

"Oh you are," Hannah replied hurriedly. "Perfect."

All words were lost to her when he came over her, the weight of his large body somehow feeling just right.

Hannah dared to slide her hands down his back, loving the fact she had every right now to touch every inch of him. So strange that although his skin was soft to the touch, at the same time, there was hardness underneath.

The feel of his hands moving up her sides to cup her breasts made all thought evaporate. Then his mouth covered one tip, taking her in and suckling gently each time sent rivulets of heat down the length of her body.

So lost was Hannah in him that when his hand moved between her legs, she barely noticed.

"Ah!" she called out.

The combination of his mouth moving from one breast to the other and the sliding of his fingers between her sex sent the room reeling.

"I-I cannot withstand it," Hannah stammered, the flames of need lapping across her body in a way that made it impossible to remain coherent. "Please."

While at the same time clutching the bedding and kicking her legs, unable to control the reactions of her body, a thrilling fear filled her.

There was a nudge between her legs, and instinctively she knew it was his manhood. Hannah took a shaky breath and tried to remember what Felicity had said.

What had she said?

Henry's staggered breathing took her attention, and she pressed her lips against his. The kiss turned passionate, his tongue delving deep into her mouth as she suckled at it and dug her fingernails into his back.

Inch by inch, he slid into her, his hands firm on each hip. He looked into her eyes and then with one hard thrust pushed past her virginal barrier.

Hannah flinched at the unexpected feeling. It was not as painful as she'd expected.

"Are you in pain?" Henry whispered against her ear, his warm breath fanning her overly sensitive skin. "I love you."

"It does not hurt now," she replied. "I must admit, I thought there would be more to this. Felicity said you are supposed to move."

Henry chuckled. "I am so very grateful that Felicity told you what I should do next. Otherwise, this would be a rather unremarkable occasion."

Knowing he kidded, Hannah gave him a bemused look. "Well?"

Although new to what occurred, Hannah understood Henry was gentle in his movements, not wishing to cause her discomfort. He kissed her while driving in and out of her, fluid and steady.

The intimacy of the moment was beyond what she'd expected. Hannah enjoyed the closeness and feeling of his body against hers. She sighed and closed her eyes, basking in the warmth of him.

"Hannah?"

"Mmm?"

Henry barked out a loud laugh. "Did you just fall asleep?"

Immediately she was alert. "Oh goodness, I suppose I did."

Withdrawing from her, Henry lay next to her and brought her against the crook of his arm. "Sleep and rest."

When Hannah awoke, there was little light outside. She turned to Henry who continued sleeping. The fact she'd see him every morning made her giddy. She leaned over him and pressed a kiss to his slightly parted lips.

Henry's eyes flew open, then upon seeing her, his expression softened. "You are awake."

"I am so sorry I fell asleep," Hannah said. "I did enjoy making love."

"We did not exactly do anything. You were tired."

"Can you show me again what happens when you move? I am supposed to float."

His lips curved and he immediately complied, coming over her, his mouth capturing hers with so much hunger that she had to cling to him. It was erotic the way every inch of their bodies pressed close.

When his mouth traveled to her breast while, at the same time, his hands slid up and down her sides, a moan escaped from her lips. "Oh Henry."

The pressure of his hardness at her core momentarily startled her, but when he slid through the folds of her sex, the silky skin of his rod sent tendrils of heat up and down her body.

She took his mouth with greed, needing to taste him, to have more of him. Then to her delight, he prodded at her entrance. This time it was different. His body seemed to strain, as if he held himself back.

"Hannah," he murmured against her ear. "I love you."

He waited for her to adjust to his girth, his hands lazily exploring her body, tracing circles on her skin in a way that took her attention away from where they were joined.

Then he began to move, his rod sliding in and out of her, the steady rhythm of his body bringing her into what she could only describe as the most titillating of dances.

Hannah could not look away from him, the way his face transformed as he became lost in her. But moments later, she could not keep from allowing her eyelids to fall as her entire being threatened to burst.

Then it did and nothing could have prepared her for how beautiful it was.

"More. Please move more." Hannah gasped out each word.

And oh did he move. Henry took her to heights she'd never imagined.

When Henry collapsed over her, he rolled to lay beside her, his chest expanding with every harsh breath.

"You are amazing," Hannah said, turning on her side to look at him. "I do not think to ever tire of this."

"I want nothing more than to make you happy. I will strive to ensure you are always content."

A smile stretched across her face, and she trailed her fingers lightly down the center of his chest. "Will you always be as free with your body? To allow me to touch you?"

He looked at her, puzzled. "Do you know how liberating it is that you wish to do so and are not coy about it? I am a very fortunate man."

It was strange to her that after what happened between a husband and wife, someone would not feel free. However, there were instances, she supposed, especially with arranged marriages where the two were not particularly fond of one another.

"I cannot wait to explore life with you," Hannah said, leaning forward and pressing her lips to his.

They talked until dawn, not wanting to fall asleep and miss a single moment. When Henry came over her a second time, they made love in a slow, leisurely way that was as wonderful as the time before.

KNOCKS ON THE door woke them. By the light outside, it was late morning.

Henry slipped from the bed and wrapped a blanket around his waist to open the door. An older woman entered with a tray. "Tea and toast. Midday meal will be ready in an hour." Her no-nonsense ways made Hannah wonder if they were not the first to appear in the middle of the night to be married. As she walked to the door, the woman glanced at Hannah. "Good wishes to you both on your marriage."

When the door slammed behind her, Hannah giggled. "I must say, this will be a time of many interesting experiences."

Henry pulled on his breeches and then brought the tray to the bed. "Once we eat, we will return to Glasgow."

"Our friends will be glad for us. I am not sure about your mother."

His wide shoulders lifted and lowered. "She will come around. Don't fret."

CHAPTER SIXTEEN

When Hannah shivered, Henry wrapped his arm around her shoulders. "You're nervous." It wasn't a question because he too wondered about the reactions that would greet them upon arriving in Glasgow.

His parents, he didn't really need to guess. While his mother would be most put out and demand his father do something, Lord Campbell would be secretly pleased that Henry took his advice.

At the thought of his social equals, it surprised him to not care what they'd think of Hannah or her circumstances. If ever any kind of rude remarks were made, he would see that the person was sorted out. Not in a violent way, but with a personal visit asking that they repeat what was said to his face.

"What are you thinking?"

"That our friends will be pleased when we give them the news."

Hannah nodded. "Felicity and her mother will be upset that they did not get to plan and attend our wedding ceremony."

"We can always have a celebration," Henry suggested. "I was also considering that we must decide where to live. When I made up my mind yesterday, I bought a townhouse near the center of the city, and not too far from Evan and Felicity. I had my things taken there. Now that I have a clearer mind, I wonder if you would prefer to remain in your house."

A slight furrow appeared between her brows. "This is a new

start for us, Henry. My house has wonderful memories of growing up there. There are also the memories of finding out Father was killed and Mother deciding to leave. I wish to move and sell the house."

"You haven't seen the house I purchased." Henry chuckled. "I must admit, I haven't walked through the entirety of it either."

The last days had been, in his estimation, the most excitement he'd ever had. He'd finally seen that for years he'd been idling, not living up to his full potential. Even after recovering from all the gambling debts and heaviness of it. It wasn't so much that he lived in the family home, but more that he allowed his parents, especially his mother, to run his life. Mostly because he felt guilty for what he'd put them through.

After all the years of uncertainty, Hannah had brought out the best in him. The will and need to better himself. That was what true love did to a man. Something that he could never describe to another person, but that he wished for those he held dear.

"What about your mother?" Hannah's voice trembled. "She will never forgive me for this."

Henry quickly pressed a kiss to her temple. "Mother will begin the work of ensuring society accepts you. To everyone, you will appear to be doted upon. I ask that you go along with it if you can. It will help a great deal toward a relationship between you and her."

"And in private?" Hannah asked. "How will she act toward me? I ask so that I can be prepared."

"Mother, although strong-willed, and sometimes arrogant, will never mistreat you. Once you get to know her, you will realize that for all her exterior display of rigidity, she is not unkind."

"I do wish to get to know her better. Once we have children, I do not want them to feel any kind of insecurity when it comes to their grandmother."

Henry chuckled. "Mother will turn to pudding upon holding

our first child."

The carriage slowed. Outside, people scurried to do whatever they planned that day. A group of men were gathered outside the Grant Hotel, and he studied them, recognizing a few. They were no doubt meeting to discuss the upcoming elections.

"I have never asked," Hannah said. "How do you spend most of your days? Do you go there?" She looked through the window.

"I meet with Miles and Evan there often. We used to meet at Evan's house, but since he married, we do not wish to intrude. We discuss our upcoming business dealings, social issues, and of course politics."

She smiled at him. "Felicity told me about the sponsorship of the ship. She thinks you each planned to come up with money by ways of a woman. And that you are wagering against one another."

Her soft giggle made him smile.

Hannah met his gaze. "I have no money to help you with, therefore, are you going to lose your opportunity, Mister Campbell?"

"I have the money," Henry countered. "And yes, falling in love with you caused me to lose the wager. I am officially out of the game."

"I suppose Evan is still in competition since Felicity's dowry was substantial."

"You do not think that is why he married her, do you?"

Hannah shook her head. "Of course not. It is obvious he is madly in love."

"As am I with you."

They arrived at Hannah's house and Henry accompanied her inside. She planned to bathe and change before they went to visit his parents.

While she went upstairs, Henry waited in the parlor.

Marta brought him tea and gave him a pointed look. "Although I am glad that you married my lass, Mister Campbell, I hope you realize it was by most unconventional means."

"I do, Marta. I promise to make her happy."

"I must also inform you that I plan to remain by her side to ensure it."

Henry nodded. "I would expect no less."

"Are you to move in then?" Marta seemed to realize she overstepped. "I do not mean to be disrespectful, just that I wish to ensure all is prepared."

"No." Henry met her gaze. "We will all move to a house I recently purchased. You, the new housekeeper, and Silas, can begin packing. I am sure my wife will give instructions about what she wishes to take."

Hannah appeared moments later, and his breath caught. She'd changed into a soft cream-colored dress that accentuated her coloring and lovely long neck. Her hair had been brushed up and with a ribbon that matched the dress weaved into it.

A simple pearl necklace decorated her throat and she'd donned rose-colored gloves.

"I am ready," she said, meeting his gaze. Upon noting his admiration, her cheeks pinkened.

"You are breathtaking," Henry said, taking her hand. "I cannot believe you are my wife."

"I could say the same about you," she replied. "The most handsome man in Scotland is now my husband."

IT WAS APPARENT that his parents were not surprised at their announcement. His mother gave her husband an accusatory look, telling how well they knew one another.

"Well it is done now." His mother first looked at him, her expression stoic, but remarkably, it softened upon looking to Hannah. "Welcome to the family, dear."

Hannah's soft gasp made his chest tighten. When a tear slid down her face, he could not take it and grasped her hand.

"Th-thank you," she replied, her voice almost a whisper.

As expected, there was a gleam in his father's eyes when he stood and pulled a cord for a servant to come. Upon the butler's appearance, he smiled broadly.

"Horace, bring bottles of the best champagne and ask the staff to come. We have something grand to celebrate."

While they waited, his mother inquired about where they would live.

"I certainly expected that upon marrying, you would bring your bride to live here," Mrs. Campbell protested when Henry told him about the house he'd purchased.

"That house is practical, but not a place where the future Campbells should live. Goodness, Henry, if you do not wish to live here, at the very least move into the Ravenscraig house."

Hannah turned to him. "Where is that house?"

The second family home had remained empty since his grandparents had died. Although a beautiful structure where they stayed on occasion, he'd thought his father had sold it.

"It stands empty, with only a minimal staff. I use it when someone from the Highlands or England comes for business. A hosting place, as it were," his father explained. "Some people I prefer not to stay here."

"The house is in Bishopbriggs." Lady Campbell answered Hannah's question. It is almost as large as this house, but in a way, statelier. The only reason we did not move into it was because I fell in love with this estate."

Hannah looked to Henry. "I would like to see it."

Although he'd not considered the house, upon thinking about it, it was a good place to raise a family and begin life with Hannah. Upon remaining as the sole heir, his father now insisted he return to the fold, and having to entertain, the Ravenscraig house was better suited for it.

The staff appeared and his father led the toast, announcing the marriage. The news would run through the town and upon people learning of the marriage, they would also hear of the celebration and how his parents seemed pleased. The toast was the first of what would be different ways that he and his parents would begin the process of Hannah's entrance into society.

By the look of happiness on Hannah's face, she was unaware of what was set in motion, and for it he was glad. His mother gave him a knowing look and he smiled in return and mouthed, "thank you."

Once the toast was done, the staff took turns congratulating them and left as quickly as they came.

"Should I prepare a room for you and your new bride?" the housekeeper inquired.

Henry considered what was best for the situation.

"No, they are to honeymoon alone," his mother replied with a well-practiced neutral expression. I will inform you when a room will be required."

Once they were alone again, Hannah looked to his parents. "Thank you so very much for making me feel welcome. I know this is not what you would have wished. However, I must tell you that I love your son with all my being and will strive to make him happy, always."

There was a beat of silence and his mother sighed. "It is done now, and I am glad to know how you feel. I do wish you every happiness." She straightened. "There is much work to be done in the days ahead."

"Mrs. Murray would like to be involved," Hannah suggested. "It would please her greatly."

"Good."

AFTER WALKING THROUGH the house Henry had purchased, they decided that, along with Hannah's, it would be sold.

Although Hannah liked the townhouse, it was imperative to keep the family happy. Living in Ravenscraig would be affirmation that the marriage was accepted and approved by the Campbells and be another stepping stone to stopping some of the rumors and any social damage.

Although Henry understood that Hannah did not care about the elite class's social rules, she did care about the effect on his family, and therefore, was agreeable to do as much as possible to keep his mother happy.

"I hope you like the house," Henry said to her as they sat in the townhouse's dining room sharing a meal with their friends.

Somehow between Marta and the new housekeeper, they'd managed to produce a four-course meal along with a delicious bread pudding for dessert.

"You must show me the house," Felicity told Hannah. "If you are to leave shortly, perhaps I can help find someone to purchase it."

"We have two houses to sell," Hannah replied. "Hopefully they will sell easily."

Grant cleared his throat. "I would be interested in purchasing this townhouse. It is accessible to many things, and it is time I move into a place of my own."

There was an awkward silence, as no one wished to bring up the subject of money. Of course being Grant's sister, Felicity had no such compulsion.

"How exactly will you pay for it, brother?" She gave him a pointed look. "If you can afford this house, then you must be hiding something from me."

He, along with Evan and Miles, avoided looking at each other. Unfortunately, it only made the women more curious.

"What are you hiding?" Hannah asked, looking around the table.

Felicity's eyes narrowed. "I will find out even if you do not dare tell me, Grant."

"If you wish to purchase the house, be sure to let me know before I contact an agent," Henry said, ignoring both Hannah and Felicity's questioning looks.

"About your family home. You may wish to wait," Evan told Hannah. "There have been many changes right away. I advise that you wait and see how you feel about selling it after a few weeks have passed."

"What would I do with it until then?" Hannah asked. "I have no family, and although it could bring me rental income, I am not sure to wish to be involved with having to oversee it."

As the conversation whirled around them, no one seeming to be eager to leave, Henry relaxed and considered that in the present moment, he was experiencing the most perfect day of his life.

Finally, it was decided both the townhouse and Hannah's family home would be placed on the market.

CHAPTER SEVENTEEN

AT FIRST SIGHT, Hannah considered Ravenscraig to be a rather underwhelming house. It was square with a four-poster portico over the front door. There were five large windows on the second floor and two on each side of the front door on the first floor. Admittedly, the grounds were large and well maintained.

Upon entering, the house became more appealing. Just inside the front doors was a sitting room with chairs for visitors to be ushered into. Walking straight forward, the entryway opened to a splendid foyer from which one could spot a large parlor to the right and to the left, a dining room and a large open space, which could be used for hosting a ball.

Straight ahead was the staircase, a beautiful creation with marble bannisters that widened as it cascaded onto the floor, creating the allure of welcome.

The house was bright with sunlight at the moment, but from the large intricate sconces and candelabra set on different surfaces, the evenings would prove magical.

There was already a staff of four at the house, who'd been hired by Mrs. Campbell. By their earnest expressions, they were eager to bring service and prove their worth. Soon there would be a pecking order of who would do what and Hannah looked forward to seeing to it.

No sooner had she and Henry walked through the house and selected which bedchamber would be theirs did Marta appear from the back of the house.

"A pair of wagons has arrived," Marta said, hurrying past her to the front door. Once opening the door, she called out for the men to round the house to the back."

Marta gave Hannah a happy smile. "Where would you like the trunk from your bedroom and your father's desk to be placed?"

"The desk and bookshelf in the empty room at the top of the stairs to the left. Have them put my trunk in our bedroom, please."

When Marta went to see about the delivery, there were knocks at the front door. Hannah considered that she'd have to see about hiring a butler. A maid hurried past to the front door.

Moments later, the same maid came to where she sat in the parlor adding to her list of things to do.

"A Mrs. Macleod and Mrs. Murray here to see you, Mrs. Campbell."

"Please show them in. From now on when they come, they are to be shown in promptly."

The maid curtsied. "Yes, Madam."

She, Felicity, and her mother spent the afternoon walking through the house and adding items to be done to Hannah's already long list.

"I cannot wait to see how much this house will blossom," Felicity's mother exclaimed when they finally sat in a small sitting room from which they could look out through the large windows to the front lawn. "It is a beautiful home."

"I agree," Hannah said with a sigh. "There is so much to do. This weekend is an intimate family gathering when I am to meet the extended family. Then the wedding gala at the estate will be held next Saturday. Of course, I have to help Mrs. Campbell, which will leave me little time for the house."

"You have all the time in the world, and we will be helping with the gala and of course with the house," Felicity said with a wide grin. "Mother and I just finished my house, so we have plenty of experience."

"True," Mrs. Murray agreed.

By the time her friend and her mother left, Hannah was calm. "Marta." She walked to find her. "I am going to my family home to walk through once more. Someone has already offered to purchase it."

"Should I accompany you?" Marta said, but by her expression, she did not wish to.

"No. Silas is there. I will be fine."

Upon arriving at the house, it was as if a sense of peace came over her. The familiar did that, she supposed. Since she'd decided to leave most of the furnishings, upon entering it was as if she still lived there.

Barks sounded and Betty raced to her, entire body wagging side to side. Hannah lowered to pick her up. "I have been neglecting you, little one." She pressed a kiss to the furry head as the dog wiggled in excitement.

"She has been well taken care of," Silas said, appearing from the direction of the kitchen. "Do you notice she's fat now, Miss…er Mrs. Hannah?"

The pup was indeed quite plump. "I am afraid she's become more attached to you than to me," Hannah replied with a smile. "Thank you for caring after her. I am going to walk through one last time. Mr. Campbell informed me this morning that someone has already offered to buy the house."

Taking a notepad and pencil from her bag, she walked into the parlor. The small table in the back of the room had remained, as they'd decided it suited the room. When Hannah turned to the front, she pictured the times she and her parents had spent in the space. Most times, they'd each been quiet, Hannah reading, her mother sewing, and her father going over figures in a ledger he brought from his study. If only she'd realized how precious those times were, that in a blink of an eye, they'd disappear, never to happen again.

Above the fireplace there was a painting, a floral depiction of a vase with lavender flowers. The day it had been hung, her mother had cried. It had been a wedding anniversary gift from her father.

She noted that it would go to the new house.

"Hello, Hannah." A man's voice made her jump and Hannah whirled to find that Jules had entered. "The front door was open."

Despite everything, she was glad to see him. "I am in the process of moving out." She studied her half-brother for a long moment. "Why are you here?"

"I saw the carriage and decided to stop. I hoped it was you who was here."

"Why?" She looked to the doorway where Silas stood and waved him away. "I am fine."

Jules's gaze moved to where Silas had stood. "I am glad to see you have someone to keep you safe."

They would perhaps never get to know each other in a way lost siblings did. Hannah wasn't sure how she felt about Jules. A part of her wished for a relationship, but then she wondered how detrimental it would be to her new family.

"I am here to go through one last time and ensure to take what I want. I am torn about some things, as I know they will be out of place in my new home."

He came and stood next to her to study the painting. "Like this?"

"No, I am taking this one. Father gifted it to my…our mother one anniversary. It will be displayed at my house. It is small items like this." She motioned to a black and white sketch of two hands, fingers intertwined. "I never understood why this was so special to mother."

"I do," Jules said, walking closer to it. He pointed to a scribble on the bottom right and Hannah neared.

The initials instantly stood out. *"H.B."*

"Oh." Hannah's mouth fell open. Through all this, her mother had kept something from her first relationship.

"Father was artistic," Jules said, still looking at the sketch. "I have several pieces he did. Most of them like this, devoid of color."

"Why so stark?" Hannah asked.

"He was colorblind."

In that moment, Hannah realized she wanted to know more about Jules. To know about her mother's life prior to marrying her father.

"Would you like to go with me to visit Mother?" Hannah wasn't sure why she'd asked and if it was the wise thing to do. What she did know was that perhaps, them coming together to see her would ease the burden and help her mother recover.

Jules let out a long breath and seemed to consider it.

"I believe it would help her. She is not well, is overburdened with guilt."

Instead of a reply, he walked to the French doors. "I have always wanted a garden. Not sure if I can keep it as nice as in its current state."

"You are who offered to buy the house."

Jules nodded, his gaze sliding to her as if to ascertain if she was pleased or not.

"Did you have my father killed?" Hannah's throat constricted.

"I did not wish it to happen. It is my fault that it did."

A tear trickled down her cheek and she brushed them away. "I am not sure if I can ever forgive you."

"I understand," Jules replied. "Know that I am so very sorry."

They stood next to each other looking out, not speaking.

"I will go with you if it helps our mother." Jules finally replied. "To assure her what happened was not her fault."

Hannah wanted to hit him, to demand that he turn himself in. However, she knew he would not. Instead, she nodded. "Good."

"I WILL NEVER forget the look on Mother's face upon realizing who he was," Hannah told Henry days later. "It was as if a veil fell, and she could see clearly. She cried, well, we all cried. I thought Jules would be unmoved when she begged for his forgiveness for abandoning him. But instead, he crumbled immediately. He'd held so much pain and resentment toward her, but when she explained how she feared Horace would kill her, and in turn him, Jules understood why she felt forced to give him up. I felt like a third party watching a play. It was beautiful and quite sad at the same time. So many years wasted. My father's life the price."

"I am glad you went." Henry took her hand and led her from the parlor up the stairs.

"How did Horace Brown come to find Jules?"

"When he was about ten, my mother's sister brought him to Glasgow and left him with an anonymous note at Horace's house."

Henry looked at her. "Are you planning to see him again?"

"No," Hannah said with a sigh. "Father died because of him."

"We need to get some rest. There is much to do tomorrow," Henry reminded her.

"Ah yes, the gala event of the year." Hannah shivered. "So many emotions in a matter of days. I am not sure how to withstand it, except that we are together and that gives me strength to face anything."

The bedroom was one of the first rooms to have been redecorated in colors of green and soft mauve. The plush bedding was one of Hannah's favorite things, and the beautiful deep green drapes that cascaded from the windows to the floors gave the room a soft elegance that invited a person to linger.

Behind a screen, she removed her gown and donned a nightgown. Sitting down before a mirror, she brushed out her hair while watching Henry undress.

He'd sat to remove his boots and stockings, then stood and unbuttoned his shirt, pulling it up over his head.

"Your valet has been most put out that you do not require him at night," Hannah said with a smile, watching as he folded the shirt carefully and placed it over the back of a chair.

"In the morning is good enough," Henry replied, bending to set his boots next to the same chair. Hannah smiled, noting he did just as his valet would.

It was hard not to admire the expanse of exposed chest and wide back. The way his muscles flexed with every movement was mesmerizing.

"Would you like some brandy?" Henry asked.

"Yes."

Her fingers did the nimble work as she raked the hair back and began to braid it in a single plait. All the while she kept an eye on the handsome man, who poured brandy into small glasses.

Hannah stood and met him halfway to take the glass. Their eyes met as they swallowed, the fiery liquid racing down from her throat to her chest.

The heady mixture of the drink and anticipation of Henry's touch made her eager to get into bed.

"Come to me," Henry said, extending his hand out to her. "I cannot wait to hold you again."

Her stomach tumbled and she inhaled. The room smelled of burning fire, lavender, and brandy.

"I love the smell of your hair," Henry said, his cheek pressed to hers. "The taste of you."

Of their own volition, her eyes closed, and she wrapped her arms around his midsection. How had she possibly thought that it was possible to forget this man? When she'd expected he'd marry someone else, her heart had been shattered. It was only now that not only was it repaired, but full of love.

He lifted her and carried her to the bed from where she watched him finish undressing. Since Henry preferred to undress her, she did not remove her gown.

Finally, he joined her in the bed and took her mouth with eager passion. Hannah reveled in each kiss, every touch of his hands on different parts of her body. The discovery of sensations sent her reeling.

"Roll over," Henry whispered, helping her to do so, all the while his mouth pressing kisses to her shoulders and neck. "I want to show you something different."

On her stomach, she gasped as his lips trailed slowly down from between her shoulders to the small of her back. His hands caressed the orbs of her bottom, fingers tracing circular patterns on her skin. All the while, he licked and nipped at the same time.

Although Hannah wasn't sure what he was about to do, she was too crazed with passion to care. All that mattered was that he did not stop.

Hands on her hips, he lifted her to her knees, pressed himself against her, and then he slid into her. With excruciating slowness, his thickness filled and stretched her sex. When he was fully contained, he reached around and slid his fingers between the folds of her nether lips, sending heat up and down her body.

"Oh!" Hannah exclaimed, pushing back against him, urging Henry to take complete control and do as he pleased. "Yes."

Once again, he took her by the hips and began driving in and out.

"Tell me how you feel," Henry urged. "Am I hurting you?" His voice was deep and gravelly.

Hannah looked over her shoulder to see that he held back, the muscles of his neck and shoulders tense.

"I want more. It feels wonderful." She clutched the bedding in expectation and Hannah was not disappointed in the least.

With each thrust, Henry seemed to drive deeper. The sounds of skin against skin were so erotic to her ears that she could not keep from allowing passion to overtake.

"Yes! Ahhh!" Her cries floated overhead, mixing with Henry's grunts as he continued to take her so hard that the bed rocked beneath them.

Minutes later, Hannah collapsed onto the bed, and Henry covered her, wrapping his arms around her body as he continued to plunge into her, all control lost.

First to climax, Hannah's body shattered, stars forming in the darkness floating around as she lost control.

Still Henry continued, his body seeming to have a mind of its own, not allowing that he stop until the ultimate climax. He plunged into her pliant body, bringing her back to reality. But all she could do was enjoy the moment, her body too weak from her own release to move.

His rod was still hard, body tense, and suddenly, he shuddered with a husky cry as he spilled.

They lay joined for a long moment, both struggling to regain their breath. Basking in the intimacy and beauty of the moment, Hannah took Henry's hand and lifted it to her lips.

The kiss on the back of his hand almost brought tears to her eyes. She could not imagine loving anyone more than the man she lay with.

CHAPTER EIGHTEEN

UPON ENTERING THE grand ballroom at the marriage celebration, every guest immediately searched for the woman who'd captured one of the most eligible men in Glasgow. Henry looked on as one by one each person sighted Hannah and were unable to find fault.

Standing next to his mother, Hannah was resplendent. She wore a creation in shades of green that emphasized her flawless olive skin. Upon her head, she wore a tiara nestled in the burnished brown waves that had been swept up into an elegant style. From her ears hung emerald earrings that had been gifted to her by his mother. Around her neck, a diamond and emerald necklace that had been her mother's. The simple design effectively complemented her long graceful neck.

She wore elbow-length gloves in the palest green that matched one of the shades of her gown.

Once guests approached and were introduced, they'd find the new member of the Campbell clan to have flawless manners and was quite adept at maintaining a conversation.

Noting the expressions of each person upon moving away from his wife, Henry could barely contain the pride that filled him.

Lord and Lady Wilshire arrived, and he excused himself from the men he spoke to. Of anyone in their social circle, this woman had the power to ensure great social standing. If she disapproved, however, it would be hard for whoever she deem inappropriate to ever gain the good graces of society.

The couple waited to be introduced, Lady Wilshire's shrewd gaze instantly taking Hannah in.

"Lord and Lady Wilshire, my daughter-in-law, Hannah Kerr Campbell," his mother said as she'd not noticed him approach.

Upon Hannah's head bow and light curtsey, Lord Wilshire smiled. "Henry has impeccable taste. Very pretty." He patted Hannah's shoulder and turned to his wife.

Lady Wilshire's soft smile hid whatever she truly thought. "I am hopeful you are both happy," she remarked, looking from Hannah to him.

"Very much indeed," Henry said. "Every marriage should be a love match in my opinion."

"Is that so?" Lady Wilshire replied, her gaze sliding to Hannah. "Do you agree, young lady?"

Hannah looked to Henry, her gaze soft. "I wish it was that every person find who they love. However, even arranged marriages can prove successful. Love helps in the beginning; however, it is trust and friendship that makes a marriage successful over time."

"Well said," Lady Wilshire replied. "I hear you moved to Ravenscraig. Do you plan to entertain soon? I wish to see the house."

"We do," Hannah replied. "However, you do not have to wait for a social event to visit for tea. I am not experienced enough to presume to know how to decorate and value any opinion you would have, Lady Wilshire. Please do come for tea."

The woman seemed taken aback. So much so she was speechless for a long moment. The entire time, Hannah continue to be at ease, a slight curve to her lips when she looked to him.

"I am flattered," Lady Wilshire replied.

"We shall come and visit together," his mother interjected. "I may have some ideas."

Hannah clapped her hands and smiled. "I am so very glad."

As Lady Wilshire walked past him to greet other guests, she

whispered to him, "Magnificent."

As the night progressed, people danced to the music played by a well-known string quartet. Champagne flowed and trays with appetizers continually passed by servants wearing black suits.

Upon hearing loud, angry voices, Henry hurried to stop whatever happened. Just outside the doors that led to vast gardens, Grant stood nose-to-nose with a man he didn't recognize.

"Stay away from my mother," the man said, fists clenched. "I know the kind of man you are. A lowly scoundrel out to divest women of their fortunes."

Grant swung, his fist hitting the man's jaw. Although this was not the time for a scandal, Henry did not blame Grant for it. Nonetheless, he had to put a stop to it. He could not allow anything to spoil the night. He motioned Evan forward and they went to where the men squared off.

Already the guests began to whisper and watch, which of course would be the theme of the next day's gossip.

"I must ask you to leave, sir," Henry said to the man who rubbed his jaw and glared at Grant. "I do not believe that you were invited."

"My mother was," the man replied. "Lady Roberts."

The man was short with small eyes and wild red hair. He looked to be in his thirties. "Tom Roberts?" Henry asked.

Tom nodded. "Yes, we went to school together."

"I am sorry to see you again under these circumstances. I must ask that you leave. I cannot have my wedding celebration ruined."

Henry looked to Grant. "Perhaps you should go as well."

Grant grunted, turned, and went back inside. As he passed, a woman patted his shoulder and Henry wondered if it was Tom's mother. He had to press his lips together to keep from smiling. It could be his friend was about to lose the money he counted on for the ship sponsorship.

Grant remained for only a short while and then left with Miles, who'd escorted his sister. The young woman was beautiful and gaining much attention from suitors. It was comical to watch Miles' expression each time a male came near her.

That night, he and Hannah opted to remain at his parents' home, along with Felicity and Evan, whom his mother had insisted stay as well.

The bedroom suite they'd been given was large enough that both his valet and Hannah's new companion, Emma, could be there at the same time to help them prepare for bed.

As his coat, vest, and boots were removed, Henry watched across the room to where Hannah's hair was being brushed out.

"Leave it down tonight," he said. Hannah met his gaze in the mirror, her cheeks turning pink, and nodded.

Once the valet left, Hannah was assisted out of her gown. Moments later, she slid a nightgown over her arms, the fabric falling to the ground.

The young woman excused herself and left.

"You were magnificent tonight," Henry said, approaching Hannah with a glass of brandy. "Lady Wilshire's words."

Her eyes rounded. "Truly?"

"Yes. That is what she whispered to me. You made a very good impression on every single guest. No one will be able to gossip tomorrow, which I'm sure is quite off-putting."

Her soft chuckle was heartwarming. "You are wrong, dear husband. Grant Murray and Tom Roberts's brawl will be buzzing on everyone's lips. The reason for their argument and why Grant hit the man." Nearing the bed, she turned to him. "Who was that man? What happened? Tell me."

"Very well." Henry waited until they climbed in bed and Hannah settled in the crook of his arm, her head on his shoulder.

Despite the fact Hannah knew about the ship sponsorship, he wasn't sure if she knew the details of how each of them were to come up with the money. It was not his place to say anything about his friend's plans. He considered that once married, the urge to share everything was strong. Yet, he would have to learn the boundaries of it.

"It seems Grant traveled with a woman called Lady Roberts. The man with whom he argued with was Tom Roberts, the woman's son, who is not at all pleased."

Hannah traced lazy circles on his chest. "I can understand. Grant must be much younger."

"I am sure that plays into it. Also, Lady Roberts is very wealthy, which means she paid for everything."

"Whatever Grant is seeking, he will not find by continuing courting older women." Hannah pressed a kiss to his jaw. "Why does he?"

"Grant is not ready to settle. I believe he enjoys the company of older women and not worrying about the possibility of being tied down and forced to marry."

As they fell asleep, Henry looked forward to speaking to Grant to see what exactly occurred.

THE LOBBY OF the Grant Hotel was busy when Henry and Evan walked in. Luckily, Miles had arrived early and procured a table in the far corner where they could have a bit of privacy. As he passed, several men nodded in greeting; two approached separately to congratulate him on the marriage.

By the hearty congratulatory expressions, Hannah's approval was universal, and it pleased him.

"There you are," Grant said as they neared and sat. "I was wondering when the rest of you would come and join Miles in telling me how to run my life."

It was apparent that Grant was not in a good mood, so neither he nor Evan commented. Instead, Evan ordered drinks for all four when the server approached.

"I must congratulate you on your wife's successful entry into

Glasgow society," Miles said, holding up his glass when theirs was delivered. "You proved me wrong."

They toasted. "I am glad to prove you wrong in this instance, although there is yet the matter of her half-brother. His purchase of her family home may cause curiosity."

"It is not known that they are related," Miles replied.

"It will be seen as him wishing to start a more respectable life," Evan countered. "I do not think there will be a problem."

At Grant's grunt, they looked to the front door. Tom Roberts walked in with another man.

"Am I to assume his mother is cross with you for hitting him?" Henry asked.

Grant shrugged. "She assures me our relationship has not changed. I will have to see."

IT WAS LATE when Henry arrived home. The house was dark except for a lantern on a table in the foyer. Upstairs, he spotted more lights and assumed Hannah probably was in the sitting room or in their bedroom.

Entering the kitchen, he was surprised to find his wife standing over the stove. She turned to him, startled. "I am making toast and warming up stew. Tea at Lady Wilshire's was a disappointment."

"Why?" He neared and kissed her. "She is well-known for her lavish spreads."

"The theme was foreign delicacies. No matter how garnished, I will not eat a snail." Hannah shuddered. "Or frog's legs."

He walked closer and peered at the simmering pot. "It smells good."

"You've already eaten." Hannah gave him a menacing look. "I am not sharing."

While she ate, he told her about the men who congratulated

him, liking when she smiled at the news.

"Hannah, feel free to invite any friends that you wish here. I do not want to be exclusive like my parents."

She smiled. "I do have a few people from Father's office I would like to have for tea."

"This is our home, yours as much as mine. You can invite whoever you wish."

There was a softness in her expression when she looked at him that made Henry feel like a hero.

"Stop looking at me like that or I will ravish you here in the kitchen. Our bedroom is much too far."

The sound of her laughter filled the room. "I cannot imagine the look on Marta's face if she were to walk in upon us."

When her gaze moved from his eyes to focus on his mouth, Henry rounded the table and leaned down to press a kiss to the side of his wife's neck. "We may have to find out."

CHAPTER NINETEEN

"GRANT." HIS SISTER waved to him across the new coffee shop that had opened in the same location where the previous owner had been killed. It seemed morbid to him, but then again it was a prime location.

Along with her companion, Felicity sat at a table near a window, and he lowered across from her.

"Why don't you go to the market, Ana?" Felicity said. "I will stay here with my brother until you return. Take your time."

When a woman at another table slid a look in his direction and then began talking to the other three with her, he ignored it. Long ago, he'd stopped caring about society's rules and what people should or should not do.

His sister looked around and lowered her voice. "You have not come home. I wished to speak to you about the other night." She then whispered, "Where have you been?"

"I've been staying at Miles's house."

"Miles?" Felicity replied, looking uncertain. "His family is hosting you?"

He shook his head. "Not that you should concern yourself, but no. I have been his guest at the townhouse in town."

"You should repair things with Father. Then you can purchase a home of your own. Are you seriously considering purchasing Henry's townhouse?"

A woman approached and poured tea. "Is there anything you would like to eat?" she asked pleasantly, her voice just above a whisper.

Grant wanted to lean in and hear her speak more. If he were to marry, it would be someone who worked for a living. Someone who did not expect anything from family or had to sleep with someone in order to have things. A woman more valuable than him.

"Two scones please," Felicity replied, as he'd remained silent.

The woman looked at him; there was kindness in her eyes as she smiled and nodded.

What had he been thinking? He did not deserve a woman like that.

"I do what I have to do. It is doubtful that Father would have me back. He barely tolerates my presence when I visit. And now, I cannot purchase the townhouse at the moment."

Felicity had something to tell him; otherwise she'd have not sought to speak to him alone. One thing about his sister, she rarely held back and spoke her mind on matters. He both admired and disliked that about her. Especially when he was the target.

"The other night," Felicity began in a low voice, "you and that man Roberts caused a spectacle. Is his mother who you traveled with?"

"It is." Grant bit down, not wishing to show annoyance in public. "Why?"

"Henry and Evan know him. They went to school with him. Our father handles the Roberts' accounts."

"Are you sure?" He leaned forward. "How do you know this?"

"I visited home yesterday. Father mentioned it, hoping it wouldn't affect things."

Grant sat back and let out a breath. "I will do what I can to make amends."

"I would expect nothing less." His sister gave him a warning look. "Father should not have to pay for your…pursuits."

UPON RETURNING TO the townhouse, he found Miles pacing in the front room. The lord wore high boots and seemed to be seething.

"What happened?" Grant said, going directly to the sideboard to pour two drinks.

His friend met his gaze. "I was invited to a dinner. One that I did not wish to attend. Mother accepted the invitation for me."

"What is so horrible about it?"

"The woman, Louisa Kent, whom I have been pursuing, was there. With a man." Miles's jaw clenched. "To make matters worse, the hostess assumed I was there to court her daughter."

Grant could not keep from chuckling. "Quite a conundrum."

"I would have clarified things, except that it was impossible to do so without embarrassing the hostess, and in turn, her daughter."

"Not a good week for us. I've probably lost the money by fighting with that idiot Tom Roberts."

Miles had plans to one-up him and it was curious that he seemed to have forgotten it at the moment. Something about the evening had affected him in an unexpected way. Either he'd fallen in love with the widow Louisa, or the young daughter of the hostess had made an impression.

"What happened?" Grant asked as he stood to prepare for bed. "Perhaps you can woo the widow away from the man she came with."

When Miles did not reply, Grant turned. "What happened?" he repeated.

"I am to escort the young woman to a social party at Louisa Kent's home."

At this, Grant could not help but laugh. "Ah. Just out of curiosity, who is the young chit you have to parade with?"

"Freya Sinclair."

Grant stopped at the bottom step and gawked at his friend.

"She is astonishingly beautiful. Every gentleman of suitable age has tried to court her. Why would her mother ask you to?"

It was comical when Miles gave him a droll look.

"Ah yes, that's right," Grant said. "You are titled, wealthy, and from what I hear, quite handsome. You are what is considered the perfect catch."

Miles paced to the window to peer out into the darkness. "I do not plan to marry anytime soon, and therefore, must find a way to ensure not to hurt her opportunity to find a husband. To be rejected by me would ruin her."

"Then ensure she rejects you."

His friend turned to look at him, his lips curving. "Perfect idea."

CHAPTER TWENTY

WHEN THEIR GUESTS arrived, Hannah could barely breathe. It was the first time that she and Henry hosted, and she'd fretted all day over every detail.

Thankfully, both Felicity and her mother had come early that day and helped, giving her time to ensure the food was done to perfection.

Marta had been overly excited and had accidentally burned her hand. Now as the food was served, she remained in the kitchen with her hand wrapped, still barking out orders.

The main rooms of the house were ready for company, there still was much work to do, but with gleaming floors and bright candlelight, at first view, the house would impress.

It was not a large gathering: Henry's parents, her parents, Felicity, Evan, and Grant. Miles arrived with his sister, both stunningly attractive. Hannah immediately loved Penelope who, unlike her brother, was lively and talkative.

Henry's sister Alana, having just given birth, was absent.

As the guests arrived, Hannah could barely keep from shivering. Henry neared and handed her a glass. "Drink it. Stop fretting, everything is perfect."

Was it? Never in her wildest dreams did she expect to end up hosting a lavish dinner to which such highly esteemed people would attend. And to live in such a grand house with the most handsome man she'd ever met was like a fairytale come true.

The Campbells arrived; her mother-in-law took in the space

and looked to her. "What you have done in such a short time is impressive. I am not sure you require my assistance with décor."

The compliment made her chest expand with pride. "There is much to do, but the flowers and paintings are good at covering up certain things."

To her surprise, she and Mrs. Campbell were becoming quite close. The woman was disappointed if ever Hannah could not come and have tea. It turned out Henry's mother had a quick wit and was quite funny.

Felicity's parents arrived, followed by Felicity and Evan, who entered with Grant.

When the bell rang for everyone to go into the dining room, Henry approached her, and she slipped her hand through the crook of his arm.

"You are flawless," he whispered into her ear as he assisted her.

She turned to him, their lips a hair's breadth apart. "I love you."

"And I adore you."

The clearing of throats was followed by chuckles as she was sure her entire face had turned a bright red. She had never been happier.

THE END

About the Author

Most days USA Today Bestseller Hildie McQueen can be found in her overly tight leggings and green hoodie, holding a cup of British black tea while stalking her hunky lawn guy. Author of Medieval Highlander and American Historical romance, she writes something every reader can enjoy.

Hildie's favorite past-times are reader conventions, traveling, shopping and reading.

She resides in beautiful small town Georgia with her super-hero husband Kurt and three little doggies.

Visit her website at www.hildiemcqueen.com
Facebook: HildieMcQueen
Twitter: @HildieMcQueen
Instagram: hildiemcqueenwriter

www.ingramcontent.com/pod-product-compliance
Lightning Source LLC
Chambersburg PA
CBHW070357200726
48294CB00003B/958
* 9 7 8 1 9 6 1 2 7 5 1 4 0 *